I0567233

Intermezzo: The Interludes

The Morality Plays Series, Volume 2

Kimberly Greer

Published by Kimberly Greer, 2022.

INTERMEZZO: THE INTERLUDES

First edition. October 18, 2022.

Copyright © 2022 Kimberly Greer.

ISBN: 979-8987040706

Written by Kimberly Greer.

Intermezzo

a short, light entr'acte; a movement coming between the major
sections of an extended musical work.
~ Merriam-Webster

Book Two

Intermezzo

The Interludes

Kimberly Greer

Words & Muses Publishing

INTERMEZZO

By Kimberly Greer

Copyright © 2022 by Words + Muses Publishing LLC

ISBN: 979-8-9870407-0-6[1]

Published by Words + Muses Publishing LLC

Cover design by HMD Publishing.

Stock Photo ID: 120198175 Lisa A | Shutterstock.com

This is a work of fiction. Names, places, characters, and incidents are the product of the author's imagination and are fictitious. Any similarity to actual persons, living or dead, events, or establishments is purely coincidental.

---

1.   https://www.myidentifiers.com/title_registration?isbn=979-8-9870407-0-6&icon_type=Assigned

Dedication

To Mom. My forever Muse.
The only thing that would have made this writer's journey better would have been having you here beside me with your editor's pen in hand.
I hope I've managed to capture at least a bit of the magic you inspire.

A Moment with Truth

MY SISTERS AND I LIE on the beach enjoying the heat of the afternoon sun as the sound of memories being made and shared plays somewhere in the nearby distance. We're taking a few days away from the action in our story to relax and regroup now that it's clear we'll need our wits about us all too soon. I love this private spot of ours, its sands white and pristine, the clear blue waters of the ocean kissing the shore with passionate licks and strokes.

Any time uncomfortable truths find their way to the light, you can expect Influence to try and gain her foothold. She'll whisper words of deception masked as encouragement, maybe even as a plausible reality. Anything to help cushion the embarrassment of failure and imperfection. I don't intervene in her inner workings. But that's about to change. It *must* change.

For now, though, I'll take my rest in these few precious, enlightened moments. The sun's rays today are intense. Just as I like it. I blank my mind as my skin soaks up the comfort in the heat. I feel contentment radiating from Honesty, too, as she lies next to me, her palms facing upward as if she's collecting the rays for later use.

The two of us are in our element. But Accountability never seems to take her rest. She can't be enjoying this sun from under the shroud of that stupid umbrella. But she insists on stewing there, anchoring our good time with her sour disposition. She thinks our trip is premature considering all that remains untended and unaddressed. I try but fail to ignore her, imagining that I can will her voice away with the faint sounds rolling on the afternoon breeze, but she's determined to be heard.

"Oh my God!" I snap, fed up with her fussing, "Why are you always on some Debbie Downer shit?"

I love my sister, but candidly, she's a bit of a bore. She sees the world in such absolute terms, which I can understand these days. But, as I'm beginning to accept, she's incapable of wrapping her mind around that reality. Once you've stepped away from what's true, you're dead to her and unworthy of redemption.

I'm not sure she sees how nuanced and multi-dimensional she can be and that it can make her an acquired taste. For some, once she comes into view, it can take time to pull her into full focus. Accountability *is* a lot to handle after all. I cluck my tongue as I consider her impatience; she never has been able to wait with grace.

"I'm telling you dreamers," she snarks at Honesty and me, "until Mateo—"

"Don't," Honesty interrupts with quiet urgency, "he'll come to all of that. And you need to let him. In his own time. On his terms."

She props herself on her elbows, brings a hand to her head to sift through her softly coiling locks, and sighs. As she turns her head to study Accountability, she gives our sister her rare smile. It's plain, simple, and pure.

"Your world may still be black and white. But most of us these days," she eases her sunglasses back up her nose and returns to continue our sun worship, "we all experiment with a little color from time to time."

"Even when it means rewriting your own life story?" Accountability asks, her eyes wide behind her starlet sunglasses. She's loaded for bear, and though it's kinda fun to bring her to the edge of a hypertensive fit, I need to give her some peace. And I will. In a minute.

"Especially then," I cosign first as I flip to my stomach and prop myself on my elbows to ease her pique and end this snit.

"Sister, relax. Mateo will reconcile his truths. And as for Hedge? Well, Hedge is gonna hedge," I answer, not wanting to rot my mind with thoughts of the shameless lout of a human who continues to hide himself away now that the truth of his nature dominates the mainstream news cycle. "We know this. So what if he doesn't want you, Accountability? Fine. Now you know, and you can get over it, simmer down, and let all of this play out."

"I second all that," Honesty chimes in, peeking over to check Accountability's reaction. She finds our sister sitting on her towel, her long, bronzed legs crossed, her arms mimicking them as they rest under her bikini top. Her face shows little emotion, which means she's all in her feelings over this.

"Save all that energy for when Hedge realizes what he missed out on with you," Honesty continues to encourage her.

"And for all the others out there who think you'll tap out before they do. You know how it can get, how *you* can get when you have to wait to have your say."

Accountability huffs. She hates being ignored. Hates being silenced even more, so I have to hand it to our sister. She's taking getting shut down – by us and by Hedge – with atypical grace.

"Don't try to make me feel better about this, Honesty." Accountability turns her gaze to me. "This isn't ok. Not yet anyway. You of all people should see where this is headed, with Hedge and with your precious little love birds. She's coming to poke her finger in your eye. She's coming for you, Truth. You ready?"

It's my turn now to sigh as I weigh the gravity and inevitability of her words. Sometimes Life stress tests our resolve. I take no issue with that. What I don't need is the added chore of defusing and discrediting the doubt, deception, and disruption that Influence loves to create. So, am I ready to hear the noise she's planning to bring? No. Not really. I don't relish this rivalry and try, for the most part, not to even acknowledge it if I'm being honest, which, by now, we know I am. And so, I have no choice but to bring my head from the sand and defend my borders against her.

I've read there's no such thing as a good influence. Once she strikes, she causes you to think outside yourself, beyond your natural tendencies, making you mimic something that wasn't intended for you. She wields her power with pandemic precision, targeting and infecting with indiscriminate reach. That fact alone should make her shun-worthy. But, as we know, the opposite is true. She's as insidious as she is virulent. So, for her, there is no cure. But there is the armor of conscience, kindness, and self-actualization; stitched together, they tend to limit her success.

For now, those details can wait. I'm determined to stay in this moment and toast our hero and heroine as they finally begin embracing their truths. And I almost forgot. I need to go ahead and stuff that bee back in sister's bonnet for her.

"Of course, I'm ready. I'm strong. I'm sturdy. I'm built to last."

I give her my cheeky grin before returning my face to the sun and my back to the sand.

"And having you on my side is like having my own private stash of radioactive isotopes just waiting to be let loose. I'm not worried."

"Hmmm," she grunts before settling back on her towel at last. "If that's the best you've got, you should probably enjoy this moment while you can. It might need to last you."

She may be right. Influence will most certainly try to rewrite or defile the pages of our story. But for now, I'm happy to remain here, safe in seclusion as we wait for the next act of our saga to unfold. In the meantime, let's turn back the clock a little to when Mateo met Alexa. And, for your consideration, I've teased a couple of bonus tales that have yet to unfold.

Interlude One

With the Very Best of Intentions

WEDNESDAY, JANUARY 13
 Intercontinental Hotel, DC Wharf
 Washington, DC

ALEXA

My jaws hurt from delivering my elevator speech on repeat for the past hour while gripping and grinning with a collection of some of the most boring, most self-impressed people I've ever met in one place at the same time. *Nice, Sage. Remind me to make this the last time I let you make me do this.*

I try to keep my groans to myself as I wander around the recesses of a conference room cordoned off for the last of the day's events. For the past three years, I've agreed under threat of pestering to be one of the featured speakers at "The Death of Journalism and the Rise of Information Domination." It's a three-day gathering of any and every person with an opinion, voice, or view on the business of cultivating, sharing, and selling news and information. The faces of the social media influencers who attend might shift a bit from year to year, but there are some bedrocks within this bunch, and I'm not sure how I feel about being one of them. I mean, I have an opinion on all of this. I make my living shaping stories as a news producer. But the talks and pain points that I share with Sage were never meant for public consumption. Of course, he refuses to read that memo. He does what he wants. Always has. A lot like hosting this conference in-person in the post-Covid, big-gatherings-are-Petri-dishes world we continue to navigate with all the grace of a cow on skates.

Sage Vanucci, my dear friend and managing editor of the *Washington Post*, has taken tons of heat for pressing forward with his conference at an in-person venue, but he's justified and deflected it, pointing to all the safe practices he's imposed like requiring evidence of vaccing, encouraging those who wish to mask to do so, all while keeping a host of social media feeds hot with quips, clips, and bites of truth as the events roll by for those who prefer the virtual experience.

While I await my turn to take my place on the symposium panel, I find a vacant crevice of this hotel conference room turned green room where Sage briefs us, offers his thanks, and tries to bait us into discussions that might seed interesting storylines that will help carry whatever freeform conversation he's been cobbling together over the past two days while wandering from breakout to breakout. He's been reporting the entire time, and this panel, this collection of talking heads that I insist will never again include my likeness, is about to see the man in action as he questions, pokes, and prods us all into a discussion that won't end with the afternoon's entertainment. I full well expect to see some biting but erudite treatise on the fall of society thanks to the media in an upcoming edition of the *Post*'s Sunday magazine.

Just as Sage catches my gaze, I give him my back, deliberately refusing to join in his reindeer games. He'll give me hell for it later, and that's the fun of it. There's almost nothing better than pissing off my giant-hearted ass of a dear friend. I try but fail to hide my satisfaction and my smile as I pivot away, but my elation only grows, and it has nothing to do with the fact that I'm pleased with dissing Sage. That honor goes to the green-eyed god now standing in front of me.

"I think that's the first time I've seen your smile all day."

A ghost of a smile curves his beautiful mouth, and I'm frozen in place for a moment, my mind devoid of rational thought. The hunger in his gaze affirms green-eyed god's intentions and interest, and the heat blooming in my cheeks telegraphs mine as it threatens to travel north and fry what remains of any still-intact brain cells. He seems to look through me, straight to the heart of all I am. I have an equally intimate view into his lost, jaded, and restless soul. As I try to process all I'm seeing and feeling and resist the gravity of his pull, the best I can manage in response to green-eyed god is a cock of my head and a breathy, "I'm sorry?"

"I was just pointing out that you haven't looked happy to be here," he says, giving me a genuine smile now that knocks something inside me loose as his presence hooks yet deeper into me. I'm grateful for his comment, which smacks my ass back into reality as some former version of me threatens to melt into a blushing heap at the sight of this beautiful man and his equally gorgeous smile. With an assist from the return of my good sense, I find my lost voice along with my humility and self-respect.

"Then I'd better fix my face," I say with a small laugh and hope it comes across as more self-deprecating than self-conscious. I push on hoping to mask my suddenly awkward bearing. "Sage will never forgive me if I show him how I really feel about being here."

Something clean and bold reaches my nose as he takes a step closer and bends down to speak into my ear. "And how's that?" My eyes flutter shut, and I steady my reaction to him with a deep breath, which proves to be a bad idea when I inhale a noseful of green-eyed god along with the air meant to cleanse my nerves. I'm not sure if it's body wash or body chemistry, but I think I'm drunk on this scent. On *his* scent.

"Winston!" I hear Sage's voice booming from behind, effectively knocking my libido and green-eyed god back into place, "you're not trying to cut out are you, *tesorucio*?"

I spin around to meet his grumpy gaze and lift my chin when his eyes let me know he's not playing entirely.

"The thought had crossed my mind, Vanucci."

I give him my best cheeky smile, cheesing until he finally breaks and draws me into a hug. I note green-eyed god's interest as he watches the exchange between Sage and me. The two of us were never an item. Not really. We realized quickly that we make better friends than lovers, but to the untrained eye, it might look like there's something more there. Something inside me wants to know how deep green-eyed god's interest goes as he continues to assess us separately and as a pair as if watching a tennis match. Sage notes his presence at last and extends his hand.

"Dr. Da Rocha, again, I'm so glad you agreed to join us today after all." Green-eyed god meets Sage's proffered hand and the two exchange a firm, tight shake with undertones and messaging I'll need to decode later when I ask Sage about it. Sage glances to me and back to the god. "I see you've met my dear friend, Alexa. Whatever she's told you, it's all lies!"

We share a perfunctory laugh and dive into the high-level download about how we're all connected through Sage. I learn that green-eyed god's name is Mateo Da Rocha and that he teaches psychology at American University. He's become a campus favorite thanks to his pop-culture-focused courses. His classes typically look at how pop culture affects society, how advertisers exploit human behaviors to drive brand loyalty, and how social media can tend to manipulate, dilute, and even poison truth as it alters human behaviors. After a few moments, Mateo extends his hand to us both, offers a few niceties, and walks away. As he does, our eyes linger on each other for longer than necessary, capturing Sage's notice and fleeting disapproval. I mark it but don't raise it because I don't want to hear it. The first man to raise even the slightest bit of interest from me beyond a quick maintenance tryst or two since my ex-husband left us, and Sage decides to flip into big-brother mode.

"So, that's a no, *tesoruccio*."

I flip my head back to him, my face a perfect mask of innocence. "What's a no, Vanucci?"

"Don't play coy with me, girlie. I walked over here because the sprinklers were a second away from extinguishing the fire burning between you two. Jesus, Alexa, what the fuck?"

"I was just standing here—"

He cuts me off. "Look, I saw everything. But that one's not for you, *tesoro*. Word is, he's a major player. So what if he's a candidate for sexiest man alive?"

"Ah, so is that what this is about, Vanucci?"

"No," he says, his answer definitive. "He's not my type."

Though I'm sure many suspect it, Sage doesn't share his bisexuality with most people. He doesn't try to hide it either, but it's not on the menu of topics we discuss at dinner.

"I don't want you to get hurt, sweetheart. Tread lightly."

Something in the look I give him lets us both know I won't be heeding that advice. He chuckles to himself, mutters a slight curse in my direction, and we part ways as I go to enjoy the last few moments remaining before taking to his stage. I also need to make sure my makeup is flawless. I mean, you never know what might happen or who may be watching.

MATEO

I think I have a crush on her mind.

I sit two seats away from the exotic beauty responsible for my agreeing to sit on this panel in the first place. I turned Vanucci down the first time he approached me about participating because I tend to shy away from events like this. I don't need to hear myself talk. If that mood ever hits me, I can record one of my lectures. Simple as that. But when I saw the announcement confirming panelists – from the moment I saw her photo – I knew I needed to know her. I haven't worked out why yet because she seems the opposite of the type of woman I tend to pursue. I want no strings. Nothing deep or lasting. Yet, there's something magnetic about her that cries out, draws me in, and makes urgent the need to know who she is. The feeling only grows as I listen to her speak. I'm not sure what attracts me most: her intoxicating aura and boundless intelligence or the way she's taking down that pompous-ass Vanucci. Either way, she's got me in a trance. She's fire.

"Step back a second and let's be real," she says in answer to Vanucci's claim that PR has destroyed the integrity of the information that gets pushed to the masses. "Public relations exists to protect interests, sell stories and products, ideas. It's not magic. It's deliberate, intentional message management. The problem is that many in the game can't, won't, or don't respect the power and responsibility that comes along with being able to make the bad dreams disappear. We both know flaks who use their influence to shape what the public gets to hear whether or not the end-product is responsible or accurate. That's not new. What makes it different and dire this time is the fact that we haven't had to consider potential bad outcomes until the recent past. Shootings, uprisings, insurrections. That's because people *want* to be titillated. They *want* to be shocked and provoked and, in some cases, led to chaotic ideas that probably wouldn't occur to them otherwise. This is how bad actors seed their audience, find their consumers, and foment their poison. News outlets have the obligation to be fully transparent about how they gather their news, how well it presents whole-picture thinking, and whether their content leaves any room for catastrophic interpretations."

"That all sounds great, but it's idyllic," I hear myself speaking up before I can give any thought to whether I should. "Especially once we take a closer look at individual news organizations. Your position assumes news outlets define corporate responsibility in a uniform manner. They don't. They never will. So, your argument's objectively flawed."

She looks at me with curious, interested eyes as she considers my challenge. "Don't throw the baby out with the bath water, Da Rocha," she says, her tone easy and natural, almost as if she was expecting my challenge. And I. Am. Gone.

"You're right about the fact that responsibility looks a lot different from outlet to outlet. That doesn't absolve any of them of the need to draw bright lines between what's acceptable content and what's likely to inspire chaos. But I'll see your challenge and play my wild card. Maybe the wildest card of all. Look no further than the humans charged with running the enterprise. They're often compromised thanks to promises made to willing sponsors, expected ad revenues, alliances awaiting consecration and implementation. But if policy dictated the limits of those possibilities, we'd all be the better for it."

"And if you believe that," Sage intones as he breaks the tense connection that's finding solid footing as Alexa and I spar through our sexual tension, "You're seriously deluded. You can't be paying close attention, Winston."

She raises her chin and narrows her eyes, amused and, I think, expectant of Vanucci's come back.

"Let me deflate your sails, Vanucci," she says with a purr to her voice. "I see the game clearly. I know what *should* happen will never happen. Profits kick integrity's proverbial ass all day, every day." She scoots herself forward in her chair and uncrosses her caramel-colored legs, all sinew and definition, and plants them on the floor before shifting herself to one side so her body leans in towards her opposition.

"But that won't stop me from being the skunk at the picnic, stinking up the place with facts." She gives Vanucci a wan smile, and I know she knows she's just dropped her second Tweet of the day.

"It's people like you," she says, "with loud, dominant, respected voices that make the right people pay attention. You could use that influence to seed a change." Her head falls to the side and her full, red-stained lips pull into a small pout that takes me by surprise when I feel it between my legs.

"*You* set the example. You can call others to account by being the standard. Use those copious connects you cultivate even as you sit atop Olympus. Now *that* would shake things up."

Somewhere after her first few words, the outside world stopped existing for her. It's just the two of them, and I can tell she's used to their point-counter-point-style banter. It's sport for her, so it's no wonder he's roped her into this. She's brilliant. And I take back what I said about crushing on her. I think I'm in *love* ... with her mind, of course.

"I am but a man, Winston," Vanucci says with a smirk just as I realize I've been in some sort of pussy trance over this smart, classy, golden-eyed woman that I'm dying to get on her back.

"And you both live in Neverland," I say with a bit too much energy behind it. I probably just made myself sound like a dick, but I can't worry about it because that's who or rather what's in charge at the moment. I kick myself for not being able to shake whatever it is that's got me stuck on stupid around this woman.

"It's a nice notion that on Vanucci's word, news organizations will decide to be responsible in the way you suggest, but that does nothing to stop advertisers from relying on influence to promote messages and ideas. As long as celebrities tell us to buy the things that will help us get the girl, as long as gun-toting YouTubers can attract hundreds of thousands of viewers, which also attracts advertisers, you can't change how people regard information and publicity, not when it's designed to prey on insecurities and appeal to people's vanity."

Someone else joins in the debate, drawing an impatient scowl from Vanucci as he piles onto the reality that it's not reasonable to expect the news business to miss a chance at making more money by pushing the content that makes people tune in, follow, or buy.

"Then the only other possible solution would be to create a smarter consumer. How do we do that?" Vanucci posits with cavalier dismissal.

"Careful, Vanucci," Alexa says, the mock warning in her voice mixing with amusement. "Who are you to say who's smart and who's not? Smart about what? Instead of walking into an argument that feels like intellectual elitism, let's talk about what we *can* control. We can train reporters to be more than pretty faces chasing celebrity so they know what facts look like and can reliably present the news based on solid background instead of misinformation – or even their own advocacy. You need managers in the newsroom who can recognize and revise mistakes that lead to misinformation. And you need courageous executives who do the things they say they believe in, who can make the tough decision to kill or run with a story based on something other profit motives."

"Why don't you set the example, Winston?" Vanucci's retort draws a few claps, which quickly die back when Alexa claps back.

"What do you think I try to do each day, Sage? Some fires are beyond my authority to extinguish, especially when no one wants to acknowledge that they're burning. That doesn't mean I'll stop doing what I know is right. But it does mean that it's time to find some other way to help people learn what they can believe and what's make believe. When I've figured that out, I'm happy to show you the way, my friend."

"As if," he mutters, though the expression on his face is far more good-natured than his words or tone suggest. Either way, this must be the end of this session, I decide, as I listen to Vanucci thank the panel, the attendees, and the sponsors he roped into his vanity fest this year. I'm not at all sure what it is, but I don't like this guy. I don't like his attitude. I don't like his smugness. And I damn sure don't like his easy way with the golden-eyed siren whose moves I find myself scoping as our time here draws to a close.

This will never do.

Alexa

"Tell the boys I'll see them this weekend. And thanks again, *tesorucio*. Always a pleasure riling you up," Sage says with a quick rub of my shoulders and a wink. "And don't forget to save the date for next year!"

I stick out my tongue and shake my head. "Not happening, Vanucci. Find someone else to draw the short straw and exclude me out of your talking-head games from now on."

He laughs and shakes his head in response. "Are you kidding me? You can never back out! You signed a blood oath, girl."

"We'll see," I answer in a playful tone as I keep my face neutral. Though I'm keeping things light between us, he'll need to understand that I'm serious about that.

"We will, and I'll win," he volleys back, uncaring and unbelieving of my rebuff. But that's ok. I keep my eyes on him as he backs away and heads off to torture others. When he's finally left me alone, I take a moment to appreciate the break in activity and drop into a chair nestled beneath one of the small, round tables set up in the conference room. I close my eyes briefly and try to find a moment's peace. It might seem counterintuitive in my line of work, but I really don't enjoy being around people all that often. I try to visualize myself alone and away from this crowded, buzzing space, but my mind only wants to conjure images of the green-eyed god who's apparently decided to camp out in my brain.

This will never do.

"What won't do?"

My eyes fly open at the sound of the slightly accented baritone voice wafting around my senses. *Did I say that aloud?*

He pulls up a chair to join me before I can find the words to chase him away. See, I have a strict policy about and a singular response towards men, particularly those who interest me: tell your story walking. I'm not trying to hear it or you. Unless it's platonic in nature, I suck at relationships, so better to let opportunity roll on than to immerse myself and my emotions in a pop-up infinity pool. Sooner or later, it'll prove itself to be no more than a lovely mirage, leaving me parched, pissed, and forlorn.

Somehow, I don't think green-eyed god plans to listen. What's more, I'm not sure I want him to go away. Not really. Determination and confidence pour from him like the subtle notes of a fine whiskey. He's just the right amount of arrogant, yet he's not too full of himself. I give a small smile, trying but failing to tear my gaze from his piercing, hypnotic stare.

"It really must be time for me to leave. I didn't mean to say that. I mean, I didn't mean to say that out loud," I say in a rush, the words tumbling around each other like wildflowers in an untended field. Mortified but still determined not to let the teen girl inside me take over (too much), I turn up my smile and add, "it's just that dealing with Vanucci for more than five minutes at a time tends to make me twitchy."

I don't understand the expression on his face at first. I see surprise wash over him, his eyes brightening as he falls back into effortless confidence. His focus on me is absolute, which should be creepy. Should be.

"I wouldn't have thought that. You two seem close."

"Not in the way you're thinking," I answer quickly as I try to keep satisfaction from my lips and tone of voice. I know I shouldn't encourage this, but I'm drawn to the fire and can't resist the temptation to play with it.

"We were in school together and the friendship just kind of stuck," I say.

There. I stay in the neutral zone. Kinda. He nods and studies me a moment before readjusting in his chair and leaning forward.

"That explains the way you handled his questions, the way you two spar. It feels familiar. And it gives me hope."

The smile he gives me is open and genuine, not the cock-sure smirk of men who look like green-eyed god. I raise my brows in confusion, in part because I think he's just fried some vital synapses, but also because instinct seems to have trumped good sense and walked me straight into this.

"About what?"

"That you'll have a drink with me."

I knew where this was heading when I wandered into his wonderland. Just like Alice, I can't seem to find my way back through to the other side of the looking glass, but I need to keep trying. I guess.

"Um, not sure that's a good idea."

"Why not?" He frowns, caught off guard, I think, because he expected a yes. With looks like his, I'm sure he doesn't hear no. Like ever. He carries himself with the confidence and bearing of a man who knows his appeal – as he should. But I don't sense that he's pompous. There's also humility in the mix, and these competing facets to him reel me in even more. But I need to stand strong. I can look my fill. I just can't touch.

"Because I don't date, Dr. Da Rocha." I don't mean to be a bitch, and I hope I didn't sound like one. But I don't date. I do not date. I *do not* date.

"And please forgive me if I sound rude," I rush on before I can question my waning resolve, "not my intent." There. Hopefully, I fixed it. *Now shut up, mouth.*

Undeterred, he studies my face as if he's taking copious notes about something he finds fascinating, or perhaps a bit odd. His clear, focused attention makes me feel giddy. At the same time, I feel hunted and cornered, held captive by his will as he excavates my mind. I don't resist because I don't want to. I want him seeing every part of me, and I want inside of him. *Oh, Lord, maybe I do need a drink.*

"It's good that I'm not asking you on a date then, isn't it, Alexa?" he asks, his smile teasing now that he's done with his mental dig. Not that I didn't notice it before, but the notes of Latin heritage in his voice help seduce me into reconsideration, the cadence of his words soothing and coaxing the flight instinct that so reliably redirects my interest and my libido in times such as this. Usually. I guess that bitch is glitching today.

"I asked you to have a drink with me. And please, call me Mateo. My name is Mateo."

He moves his chair closer, the move subtle yet definitive, and the look he gives me captivates my desires and disarms my defenses. He's crowding me – literally and figuratively – and I'm not equipped to handle the many types of ways this man makes me feel. It's no chore for me to deflect attention from a man with my words. A smart quip here. A slice of snark there. I'm practiced and I'm perfect at it because it's my religion these days, this steering clear of men seeking new belt notches and ego boosts.

To be clear, I don't hate men. Not one bit. But my 15 years of marriage ended in disaster. I'm well healed from the broken heart and the anguish; I'm also well wise and wary of romantic entanglements. My approach keeps life simple by skipping the messiness that comes with falling and staying in love: Don't start none. Won't be none. Plain and simple. Sure, you're bound to throw out a few viable solutions alongside the extraneous roots to my equation for a happy life, but it leaves me drama- and pain-free, so I count that as a win. Label me the eternally unavailable chick and life goes on.

Something seems different about Mateo, though. He strips me of my wardrobe of deflections, leaving me bare and vulnerable, wanting, wanton. He's all the things that feel dangerous to me conspiring to tempt and tease, but I'm not ready to break my resistance.

"Mateo, thank you, but I don't want to give you the wrong impression."

"You won't," he replies before I have the chance to say no. "You fascinate me, and I'd like to know why. There's a bar here in the hotel penthouse, so that makes it convenient."

He's sincere and doesn't come across as pushy. In theory, that should make it easier to keep a thick, bright, neon-colored line – with 3-D rendering – drawn between us. I know better than that, and I think he does, too.

"I need to know you better," he continues as he searches my eyes. If I'm reading his correctly, he didn't mean to say those words to me, and we share a small smile over the brief, telepathic moment. He breaks the uplink so seamlessly I'm not certain I didn't imagine it as he returns to his confident, sexy, and self-possessed green-eye god-ness.

"And when the time comes, we'll have our date," he says with a wink and a smile that could charm the devil's daughter. "But first, let's talk a bit. Have a drink with me."

It wasn't a question. It was a statement laced with the confidence of predestination. He's thrown down his gauntlet, his tone daring me not to pick it up. And that is, of course, why I say yes.

"Sure, lead the way," and I resolve to play this game.

Nearly two hours and a heaping helping of sexual tension later, I'm much farther down this rabbit hole than I should be. I could blame the ambiance that swirls through this elegant and intimate bar with its moody drop lighting and comfortable, living-room style couches. Or I could own my thick infatuation with this fascinating stranger. Our conversation is light and easy. We laugh and click in the way of old friends reunited, oblivious to time and anything other than the two of us. It's attraction, yes, but there's so much more to this. He's familiar though I've known him for a handful of hours. He's like joy reclaimed when the morning at last returns. He resolves all the dissonant chords. And he threatens the careful emotion-free cocoon I've woven around my heart.

I visualize walloping myself in the head to beat back the errant thoughts taking shape, resolving instead to stay present and enjoy my drink and this time I've allowed myself with this gorgeous man, this smart, witty, gorgeous ... wait, did I say gorgeous?

As my internal struggle wages on, I discover that Mateo and Sage met at a university reception following Sage's talk on the social ramifications of the media's failure to protect the integrity of information. I learn a little about his teaching, too, and make a mental note to stalk him on Rate My Professors to see what else I can divine. Mateo, our conversation, and the lure of what we clearly want to happen conspire to seduce and cajole me into wanting, into *needing* to know more. I'm compelled by his energy as much as by his intent stare to fall into the moment, into the emotion, and follow where it leads.

But that's not happening, and I need to say goodbye. I decide at last to fumble through a weak excuse about needing to call it a day and get home to my boys. I figure that's better than trying to explain the reasons behind my refusal to entertain any hint of romantic interest.

"Aren't you tired?" he asks, making me scrunch up my nose in confusion. "Of dodging and deflecting me?"

I look away from him as my cheeks heat at the direct hit. I'm not sure how to respond.

"Look at me, Alexa."

He speaks the words softly, but that doesn't lessen their urgency. As my eyes lock with his, I find a stormy tumult in their gray-green gaze to rival the tempest brewing inside of me. He's as attuned to me as I seem to be with him, which doesn't surprise me as we ride the eye of this storm, strangely calmed and soothed by the chemistry raging between us, chemistry neither of us knows what to do with.

"You've spent so much time blocking and tackling you've got *me* tired," he jokes, venting some of the tension. He studies his mind for his next words as intently as he studies me.

"I'm just asking for a bit of your time. To get to know you a little better. A lot better if I'm lucky."

Now that's caught my attention. Though I'm tempted to give in to the pull between us, I don't do hook-ups. Not anymore. As that seed takes root, it leaves me confused and a little pissed.

"Not what you're thinking, love." His face lights with humor and maybe a bit of frustration as he reaches for his drink. "I want to know more about you. You're beautiful, Alexa. And yes, I'd love to spend time with you. What man wouldn't?" He leans in and whispers in my ear, "And for the record, I don't think one night together would be enough."

My heart races at his nearness and at his affirmation, and I'd be lying if I denied my arousal at his arrogance and determination. That potent mix is kryptonite to my resolve to get up, walk away, and remember tonight with a sigh and a smile once I get my head about me again. When he finally pulls away, we watch each other for several uncomfortable moments as my mind scrambles for ways to shut this down. Who am I kidding? I'm enjoying the attention and the flirtation more than I'm comfortable admitting. There's a glint of humor in his eyes, which see straight through to my desire.

"Some things are complex, Mateo," I say to break our silence. "Of course, I'm attracted to you. But I don't plan to do anything about it."

He returns his glass to the café table, angles towards me, and reaches for one of my hands to give it a quick squeeze before tightening his grip.

"Look, relax, and listen. I want, no, I need to know you better. I want to understand your mind. See what's behind that quick wit."

He reaches into one of his blazer pockets and pulls out a business card and wallet before flagging down our waitress, who's at our table with the check before I have time to think to say no.

"Think about it. Then meet me for lunch on Friday. Until then."

He doesn't give me a chance to respond as he leans over, plants a quick kiss to my cheek, and leaves me sitting there with my singular thoughts and racing heart.

Interlude Two

You and I, We Can't Be Friends

FRIDAY, JANUARY 12
  Tidal Basin
  Washington, DC

ALEXA

I tried to find the reasons to say no to seeing Mateo again, but they simply wouldn't come. That's why I find myself taking careful steps towards *Good Noshes by Cameron*, the food truck that Mateo chose as our meeting place for lunch.

It's only lunch. It's only lunch. It. Is. Only. Lunch. I offer myself this chant, hoping the affirmation will soothe and calm my nerves. The location's low key and unremarkable enough that it should put me at ease. Then again, I think I've been on edge from the moment I agreed to see him again. My nerves have me tugging at the shoulder strap of my purse as I near the crowds gathered by the menagerie of mobile eateries staged along Washington, DC's Tidal Basin. The selections were almost as eclectic as the District itself, so no matter your craving – wings and Mumbo sauce, chicken tibs, lobster rolls, cupcakes – odds are you'll walk away sated.

Even as I try to tell myself it's no big deal, I can't find the wisdom in agreeing to spend extended time with someone who gets under my skin enough to make me want to scratch it, examine it, and open a research facility dedicated to discovering the science behind why he does this to me. My life is neither ordained nor designed to hang on to such attachments.

It's just before noon, so each truck has attracted a steady clientele. It's impossible not to notice him towering above most everyone as he stands off from the *Good Noshes* customers, aloof and unaffected. He's pulled his inky black hair into a ponytail that rests at the base of his neck, leaving strikingly high cheekbones on full display. I witness more than a few furtive glances being thrown his way as the lunchtime foot traffic flows past. Yet, he's unbothered by it all, glancing up at me a time or two before returning his attention to his phone. As I close the distance between us, I steady myself, hoping to come across as composed even though my heart seems to have decided that it's time to start skipping around.

"Not late, am I?" I ask.

Mateo

I, along with damn near every other man and half the women nearby, saw Alexa when she stepped from her Uber. Her beauty is blinding, and she's kicked things up a notch today, making casual look classy and irresistible. The same pang that stabbed my chest the moment I saw her attacks with force and throws me off my game. I can't let her see that I'm disoriented and maybe a bit shook, so I grab at my phone and turn my attention to the screen but only after I commit her to memory.

Alexa stuns in her light blue cashmere tam, which she's placed on her head in that way stylish women do, and matching sweater with this swirling, flaring, asymmetrical hem trimmed in a band of suede. Her energy channels a European runway model, her outfit obeying every move as she walks in cool confidence in her second-skin jeans and short, high-heeled suede boots that match the trim of her sweater. Though her packaging screams confidence, her face tells a different story, a story much like mine, I'm guessing. She's wary of me, and the idea of that entertains me. Just wish I understood why.

Hearing from her wasn't a surprise. I knew she'd call because women are easy to read – especially *this* woman. Attraction is as common as water. Throw a little unreadable, untouchable energy their way, and you're good. They're yours for the taking. But Alexa is different. All women speak with their eyes; Alexa weaves epic legends with hers. I'm not easily seduced, yet she's ensnared me. She's also done something for me that most women don't: she makes me want to know more than how she looks without her clothes. I'm not sure what I want to know most, but something about her calls to me in ways I've never experienced. I feel like some social media stalker who falls for a face stuck in the moment. I know it was more than that, though. I know she's more than that moment. She's *all* the moments. I felt it when I met her, and I feel it with conviction now. I'm not saying I want a commitment. Been there. Done that. Never again. But I could be persuaded to settle in for a bit while I figure out what it is about this one that's caught my attention. I look up and stuff my phone into my jeans.

"Nah, you're not late. You're never late."

She frowns slightly and narrows her eyes. "How would you know?"

"You just don't seem like the type to tolerate lateness – in herself or others." I shrug because that's the best explanation I can give her. Real talk, it would sound creepy if I said I can read her because we're connected in some way that defies the boundaries of my knowledge. All I can say is from the moment her face jumped from my computer screen, it infected my mind and stirred interest in my heart. That last part makes no sense, though. I shut down that death trap years ago. *Didn't I?*

"Am I wrong?" I ask, finding I'm deeply interested in her answer.

"No," she answers and gives me a small smile. "But you beat me here, so I'm afraid I'm not that punctual after all."

"You're fine, and for you, I'd wait," I say as I walk into her space and drop kisses to each cheek. "It's nice to see you again. Thanks for meeting me."

She blushes in response, taking us both by surprise, I realize, as she reaches a hand to cup her left cheek, averting her eyes when she confirms the evidence of her embarrassment.

"Yeah, Da Rocha," she says, clearing her throat and calming the nerves threatening to snap and explode at my touch. "Should we get in line?"

"Sure," I say, following her lead to refocus the energy from the arcing charge between us elsewhere. "You're in for a treat."

I grab her elbow, steer us to a place in line, and give her the short history of my friend and college roommate Cameron, the rocket scientist turned food truck mini mogul. My boy's always been a foodie, but he's created some next-level offerings through his mobile eatery concept, and that's why I invested in his business. Alexa doesn't need to know *that* part, though. As Cam's mom would tell us, never let anybody see what you're working with.

We place and receive our orders and head off to find a space to sit and chat. By winter's standards, today's a warm one at 55 degrees, but the light breeze coming off the nearby man-made reservoir intensifies the chill as we scan the busy sidewalk to find an open table. When we reach one, I put down my lunch so I can shrug out of my jacket and hand it to Alexa, who's been trying to ignore the obvious chill shearing her muscular but petite frame. When she eyes me curiously, I shake my head and lean over so I can place it around her shoulders anyway.

"Don't be a hero, girl," I scold playfully with a pat to her shoulders. "I see you shivering."

Her answering smile takes me by surprise. It's the kind of smile that wipes your brain of relevant thoughts because the only ideas in my head right now concern my need to know every single thing about her. Right. This. Minute.

Alexa places the clamshell container holding her lunch on the bench, freeing her hands to close my jacket around her shoulders.

"Don't think I pegged you for the chivalrous type, Da Rocha," she says before dialing back that lovely smile. She looks down and shrugs back into that less certain version of herself that I need her to put that away. Insecurity doesn't suit her. "Thank you," she continues, glancing my way briefly before returning her eyes to her lap. "I should have dressed more appropriately for the weather."

"You're fine for walking around in the city," I say, reaching out to finger the soft wool of her sweater. "Maybe not so much near the water. It can feel colder down here."

Her smile returns then she twists her lips wryly. "Guess I don't get out much and I'm not a city dweller, so thank you again. For the jacket and for schooling my suburban ass."

We both laugh at that, then I take the opportunity she created for me once our laughter dies down. "How do you peg me?"

"I don't know," she says after studying me for a minute. "You're unreadable. I think I have you figured out, but you say something that proves me wrong. That makes me a bit nervous. Are you always this intense?"

I shake my head and eye her with amusement. "All this after seeing me twice? What? Are you a mind reader?"

She shoots me a cocky smile. "Not at all. But I *am* in the news business. Trained to spot lies and deception."

"Neither of which I'm guilty of. But if I seem intense, it's because I'm focused on you. Trying to figure *you* out. And so we're clear, you're the cagey one, girl!"

Alexa purses her lips and narrows her eyes. "Fair enough. But what are you trying to figure out, Da Rocha?"

Everything. Tell me everything about you. Help me see why I'm about to break all my rules. I don't say any of that although it's the one response that encapsulates the intensity she sees and feels. In these past minutes with her, I've imagined having her under me because who wouldn't? She's gorgeous. She's defiant. I want to tame her. But there's more than that to her, more that I want from her, and I don't know what to do with any of these urges. I don't recognize the man in control of my thoughts. Until I can sort that, I decide to drop back from what probably feels like pursuit into something more playful. Safer.

"I just want to get to know you. I don't bite. I won't kidnap you. I'm house trained, so if any of that's the problem—"

I let my words hang, my face playful and open as I angle myself to face her. Her eyes are serious and sober. She's the one who breaks our connection, turning her attention instead to the white bag containing her lunch to retrieve a wet wipe. She opens it, cleans her hands, then turns to meet my expectant stare.

"My life is complex. That doesn't leave much time for socializing, Mateo," she says at last. "And I've told you: I don't date."

I throw up a hand in dismissal and give a quick shake of my head.

"Everybody has stuff to do, so that's just an excuse. You make time for things that matter. That's all I'm asking for. Just a bit of your time."

"We all want things, Da Rocha," she says, her smile returning to let me know she's teasing. Yet, I feel the playful rebuff like a blow to my gut. "There's not much to know about me I don't think. Nothing you don't already know anyway. I work. I'm a mom. Nothing else to see here."

"No. That's where you're wrong," I say. "Tell me about your work. How'd you become a news producer?"

As expected, getting her talking about herself loosens her nerves and steers us away from the littered terrain where our emotions have lain a collection of booby traps, reminding us to keep things light, urging us instead to aim for the friend zone and stay there. Our conversation finds an easy gait as we trade stories about our work and tune out the world around us. When we finally dig into our meals, we add how kick-ass this food is to the discussion.

"This wrap is swoon-worthy," she says, her voice breathy with appreciation, which, of course, makes me think of a completely different type of pleasure, and I need a minute to find my response. I laugh and take some drinks from my water bottle.

"Do you always have such intimate relationships with your food?"

She returns her wrap to its clamshell container, grabs a napkin, and covers her mouth, her eyes wide with embarrassment before finding the humor in the moment and relaxing into it.

"So, you're a comic," she says.

"No, not me. But I feel like maybe I should leave you and your sandwich alone because I wouldn't want to get in the way."

"Yeah, yeah, Da Rocha, whatever," she says with a chuckle. "I'm just saying this is surprisingly good. Amazing, in fact."

"Yes, it is. Glad you like it."

"An excellent choice. Thank you for that. And thank you for the company."

She wants to say more but can't; her words have ushered in an awkward vibe that hangs between us and seems to stop time. Whatever is said next sets the tone for how things move forward, *if* they move forward. Determined to sway the odds in my favor, I take the lead.

"Thanks for taking time out and meeting me," I answer, adding quickly, "I like spending time with you." Simple. True. Direct. "How about we make it a thing?"

That's a bridge too far, maybe, but the words are out of my mouth before I can stop them. *What am I asking her for exactly?* Her face falls, and though I brace for the brush off, I mentally regroup because I'm enjoying the challenge.

"Make what a thing?"

"Lunch. Once a week," I say, ripping the first idea out of my head and tossing it her way. "We can make it a standing date."

She gifts me her smile once more along with a slight shake of her head. "Mateo, I don't think that's the best idea."

I nod and give her a smile because that's not a no. It's indecision, maybe a little discomfort, and I can work with that.

"I disagree. I think it's the best idea I've had all day. Besides how are you gonna shut me down before you even hear me out?"

"Mateo—"

"Alexa, listen," I interrupt her, "I don't pursue relationships. Of any kind. But you're different. I want to know why." I angle myself towards her. "I won't lie and say I don't want more," I shrug and let my declaration stand before adding, "and I know you do, too. But that can wait. Until then, let's hang out, get to know each other. That all." *For now.*

My hands go up in friendly surrender, and she studies me as if I'm an alien species. In her mind, she's dissecting me and my argument, examining both for flaws and foreign features that might require her in-depth review. I wait her out, allowing the uncomfortable silence between us to bloom once more because the ball's in her court. Finally, thankfully, she offers a small smile and a shrug of her own.

"Listen, I'm intrigued, but who wouldn't be? I'm sure most women are. And though I'm sure you're not used to hearing no—"

I lean over even more, completely invading her space. "I'm not asking for a lifelong commitment, girl. Just a little of your time."

Had I not been so close, I'd have missed the quick, sharp catch in her breathing at my words. Satisfied that I at least caught her attention for now, I lean away to leave her to her thoughts while I order an Uber to get her back to her office.

"I'm divorced with three children, and I'm probably older than you are," she blurts out, stealing my attention from the screen. "There's nothing to see here, Mateo."

It's my turn now to consider her. I can't decipher her dismissal, not because my ego won't hear of it, but because something inside knows she's making excuses instead of sharing the truth of how she's feeling. I stand and extend a hand to her.

"Walk with me."

She looks at my hand and then back to me before standing. Each of her movements is tentative as she dusts at her jeans, brushing away at nothing from what I can tell, so I write it off as a nervous tick and offer her my hand again. When she takes it, I lead us back towards the food trucks that remain streetside to wait for her driver.

"First off, our ages don't matter. We're both adults." She turns to look at me and then away again. "And second, I've told you what I want. To get to know you. For you to get to know me."

"And then what? I don't want to play games with you."

I shrug. "I don't know. But I assure you I'm not playing games."

I stop walking, reach for her other hand, and turn her to face me. I drop her hands, take a couple of steps towards her, and reach down to finger a curl dangling from her hat.

"I can't claim I understand why, but I'm drawn to you." I keep playing with her hair as I watch her for reaction. She stays silent, but I hear, feel, and see her response. When I give the lock a slight tug, her response confirms what I see. She's as helpless to the pull between us as I am, so we linger here.

"Tell me you don't feel this."

She swallows and huffs out an exhale. "How could I not? Of course, I do. But as I said before, I don't plan to do anything about it. I *can't* do anything about it."

Desire has me wanting to back her into something and kiss her senseless until she submits to what we both want. I could do that. I could *so* do that. But that would be that, and there's more to this girl. That's why I give her a small smile, release her hands, and fish into my jeans pocket for my phone. I glance at the screen and see that her driver's approaching, so I don't have much time. I also feel like she's ready to run away, which makes me to want to chase her. I'll smack myself around for that later, but for now, I need to close the deal, though I'm not sure I know what that looks like. I lean in and whisper in her ear.

"We'll talk more next time. Your ride's here."

I drop a kiss to her temple and smile when I read the confusion on her face as I take her hand again and lead her to towards her Uber. I open the car door, confirm details with her driver, and motion for her to get in. Her pace is slow and tentative, and she eyes me with disbelief.

"When we were sitting on the bench, just before we walked over," I say, filling in the blanks before she asks. She pauses at the door briefly, but the smile she gives me this time is laced with something different. It's shy and expectant. I don't know what it means. But I'm taking this as a sign that I've at least cracked her walls open enough to see what's behind the massive resistance.

I rein in the smile threatening to spread across my face at my small triumph and give her a wink as she crouches into the backseat to settle in for her ride. We say our goodbyes, and I turn to leave, knowing I'll hear from her sooner than later.

She hasn't realized it, but she's still wearing my jacket.

ALEXA

I should be ashamed of myself. *Should* be.

I knew the moment he stepped away from the curb that I was clinging to the jacket Mateo had draped around my shoulders a little over an hour ago. That meant I'd have to find a way to return it to him. We'd have a reason to see each other again.

I close my eyes and take a moment to consider how I feel about that. I enjoy the new, familiar, airy way I feel with him. I want to give in to it and get to know more. Feel more. But as tempted as I am to lean into this, I'm warned away by the fluttery feeling and the pheromonal high that visits me when we spend time together. This isn't the starry-eyed wonder or raging attraction that hits you between the eyes – and a few other places, too – when you connect with someone. It's easier, familiar, like complementary halves finding home base. He feels like permanence.

I run through what I think I know about Mateo Da Rocha. My mind plays impressions, though, not scenes or memories. No facts either because I don't have those. I know how I see him. How I feel him. How he makes me feel. *God, how he makes me feel.*

The problem with this is that I don't feel. Not anymore. I'm cured of that.

Following my divorce, I needed to remove the stains of my 15-year marriage from my conscious mind. I knew it wouldn't be a simple task or a singular act. But I also knew that my mind needed the distraction of believing otherwise. Thus was born the year of living before thinking. I took on more assignments requiring travel to places I'd never been. That meant I could do what and who I wanted. And so it was that during my year of excessive travel and extravagance, I dabbled with Roux on my trip to the French Rivera, toyed with Declan during my many visits to the UK, and dallied with the superhumanly gorgeous Prince Christos while covering news of the freefalling Greek economy. I dipped my broken heart in the salve of pleasure, exploration, and meaningless hook-ups. There was never anything more, and that was fine with me. Christos would have clung had I let him; he was so far down the path to ascension to his country's throne that he might as well have been born a Macedonian. But as with any others who tried to have more than a moment in time with me, I shut down and moved on, keeping my world tidy while my heart mended.

At the same time, I supercharged my reputation as a thoughtful news producer. I partnered with weekend lifestyles anchor Gretchen McMillan to create a news broadcast that told the news of the day alongside the dish of the day. Together, we found instant success as well as a way out of the weekend lineup. Gretchen knows and has said as much many times: but for me, she'd be laboring in the quagmire of pop culture that can stall out legitimate news careers. But I had the brains, she had the looks, and we made lots of money. The rebranded *Gretchen McMillan Show* hit hard with its mix of compelling stories, guests, and reporting team. If I had to describe it, I'd call us a mix of *The Rachel Maddow Show* and *SNL News*; for all the show's tough edges and introspection, it packed wry humor, irony, and personality into each broadcast. We became the top-rated cable news program at the 8 p.m. hour. I should be proud of that. And I am. I think. Just, maybe, I don't care right now.

I've never suffered from having a one-track mind. There's always a swirl of thoughts colliding as they compete for dominance and a path to the winner's circle. But today, competition is lacking. The clear winner is Mateo Da Rocha by several noses. Legs and arms, too. I was never the little girl who dreamed of finding and falling for her prince. I believe love is a myth conjured by the parents of old, desperate to move their children along into lives of their own so they might return to living theirs. They passed down the legends of epic love for the little ones to lap up, lock in, and one day find a suitable replica for themselves. But I never believed the legends, which is good if my dumpster fire of a marriage is any indication of the lie of happily ever after. That's why I can't let Mateo get too close. I can't seem to separate thoughts of him from epic, prince-inspired ideas.

My only choice is to extinguish this fire before it flames. I'll call Sage. He'd warned me away, so I'm certain to get him talking and scolding if I go asking after Mateo. Maybe I'll find the discouragement I'm not quite sure I want but know I need. I'm not sure what I'll do if what he shares is bad. But the more you know, right?

THURSDAY, FEBRUARY 29
    The Offices of Storey|Fischer|Stone Public Relations
    Tysons Corner, VA

ALEXA
    I hear my phone buzzing from the depths of my purse as I sit in the lobby at Storey|Fischer|Stone awaiting my discussion with co-founder Samson Stone. The stuttering pattern of the sounds, heard in rapid-fire succession, lets me know who's on the other end of this untimely interruption.
    Mateo: Stop overthinking. You said the job is yours if you want it.
    As I shove the phone back into my bag, I have the irrational urge to punch Mateo in the throat. What began with a few casual calls, texts, and meet ups for coffee or lunch six weeks ago has become what I feared. Sage was strident in his warnings to keep my emotions at a distance if I decided to spend time with Mateo, but my mind keeps forgetting to heed the warning to be wary of being seduced by the unattainable. Instead, whether by intent or instinct, I continue testing the limits of my self-restraint as Mateo and I take turns flirting with the line that separates platonic from passionate. I've come to rely on the morning texts, random calls, his pop-up visits to the studio, and all the other ways he's found to force his way onto my list of necessary things. We've fallen into a tight friendship (or is it a flirtship?), and it's almost enough to make me let down my resistance and date him. Almost.

I've come close a few times. He's a temping confection of wry humor, quick wit, sharp intelligence, and compassion. Despite his urbane sensibilities and alpha-confident indifference, he's a barely contained tempest, reined in by strength of will alone. I sense the furious energy arcing within him as deeply as I feel the gentle, generous soul at the heart of the man. *That's* the Mateo I want to know better. It's also the version he keeps to himself. So, I hold what he makes me feel close. Past hurts have a way of haunting your hopes for happiness, but I think I could banish my specters if I saw consistency in Mateo. Because I haven't, we've found ourselves trapped in a game of emotional tag. I relax. He retreats. He advances. I run away.

This time, he's gone missing. There's been little communication between us over the past couple of weeks unless I initiate it, and even then, he's been all one-word replies if he bothers to answer. Neither of us is a kid, which is part of the reason we keep circling each other. I'm wary of the gulf between our lives: I'm seven years older with three sons and little faith. In anything. The life he lives is freer, less encumbered, and, from all I can see, comes with *far* fewer worries or obligations. Don't know for sure because he doesn't let me see. Not fully. It's like talking to someone through a door. The conversation is warm and welcoming yet remote, inaccessible. It's like coming home to find the door barred to you with no way in.

Considering our radio silence, and I wonder why he's chosen now to reach out. It gives me hope to know that although he hasn't been talking, he's been listening. But if he heard me, he'd know his timing is shit. I'm feeling shaky enough about this interview, about jumping from the news business into the world of image making, shaping, and saving, without having to think of him, too. Even as my mind drowns in thoughts of navigating such a sea change at this point in my career, it's been a battle not to be in my feelings about what we mean to each other. Is there any upside to walking a path that seems to circle upon itself? His having cancelled each time we were supposed to get together over the past few weeks doesn't inspire my confidence, and I'm a lost, ill-tempered, soggy mess over it. Over *him*.

How am I supposed to interpret this? What happened to make today any different from the past few? I'm confused and angry with myself for thinking a man like him could ever want a relationship with me, this damaged, used vessel with three children. I haven't got time to slog through a mine field of complex feelings. But I'm apparently determined to do so as I retrieve my phone and reread Mateo's second message.

Mateo: Work your terms. Say yes. Then meet me for a late lunch.

Me: So glad you've got it all figured out. I'm going dark until this meeting is over. And no to lunch.

Satisfied with my reply, I return the phone to my purse and my attention to this interview where it belongs. I'll deal with Mateo of the many moods another time.

Mateo

I wander from my office with no destination. Office hours for today are nearly done, and if any of my students planned to see me, it would have happened by now. I've felt caged in here along with my growing regrets as I try to sort some of the shit I fucked up and need to fix. I feel restless, and I never am. It's taken all my strength a few times today to keep from knocking a hole through the walls, so I know it's time to vent this valve and clear my head.

I wasn't expecting her refusal, but it shouldn't surprise me either.

A couple of weeks ago, I decided to put space between Alexa and me. I've always appreciated the tease and chase in my dealings with women. But we've been careless in our interactions.

Lunch has become a regular thing for us when her schedule permits. She's often moving from place to place, and when it's convenient, Cam's lunch truck becomes our ready meeting spot. These times between us are simple. Pure. No bullshit. Just two people spending time. Underscoring each breath, each look, each of these moments spent hanging out is the attraction and burn for more. But something's holding her back, and it's clear Vanucci's been slinging shit about me her way. I don't give a fuck what he thinks or says. What I care about is the fact that Alexa is using his cautions to cement her resistance campaign, and that pisses me the hell off.

I know I can't play games with her. She's as strategic as I am with managing and shielding her heart, calling my bluff, or tossing her own lures to see if I'll bite. The challenge she issued grabbed me from the day I met her, but I don't have it in me to stay trapped in this closed loop, circling each other and our feelings because what's between us isn't casual or small – not anymore. Neither of us can take the leap of faith required to trust that trusting each other won't be the weapon of mass destruction that shreds our lives into pieces that might not fit together again. But at least I'm willing to take steps to see where this can lead. Alexa of the many masks? Not so much.

So, I'm taking a break from it. I've bailed out on seeing her, and I've been slow responding when she texted me, if I bothered answering at all. Ghosting is never cool, but I needed the space as much as I needed to do something to shake things up between us. At first, I thought I'd return some energy to rediscovering my passion for my profession. But it didn't take long to see that the well is dry, and that's a different discussion I'll have to table for now. The matter of disentangling from my university ties is a complex one. The dean of the department of psychology – my mentor, my guide, my uncle – takes a keen interest in steering my academic career. My interests, however, lie someplace entirely apart. Again, something to tackle another day.

None of my thoughts have made much sense during my self-imposed separation, which doesn't make me happy, but it's clear where my head is. I've missed her, and it's felt like I've lost a limb or vital organ. She thinks I'm not paying attention, that I'm probably on to something or someone else, but she's all I can think about. I've read and reread her messages for the past few weeks like the act itself would somehow keep me connected to her, help me know how she was doing, whether she was happy or sad. The fact that she's shutting me and herself down now, though? Nope. I wasn't expecting that.

This woman! This lovely, fragile, frustrating, stubborn woman, will kill me, and I don't know what to do about it. Check that. I know what I want; I just don't know if I can go there again, and so I do nothing.

"Hey, Dr. Da Rocha."

A flirty voice breaks through my blues as I descend the stairs to the building lobby. I can't place it because after a point, they all sound the same. The voice raises my irritation as it closes the distance between us; it's an artifact from my past and a vivid reminder of why Alexa stays rooted in her resistance. The scent of too much of a bad perfume reaches me before she does, making my foul mood worse. I brace for whatever shit she's about to shovel as she sidles up to me.

"You're a hard man to catch," she says, placing heavy emphasis on the word hard. "Got plans for tonight?"

I consider her with as much disinterest as I can summon. Attractive, short, and fit, she'd approached me at a bar one night shortly after Alexa and I met. I took out my sexual frustrations with her and turned the page. But from the look she wears, she didn't get the memo: I rarely play in the same sandbox twice.

"I'm busy. And that's not how this works." I sound like a dick, but it can't be helped. I rip my gaze away and turn to move away, but she's not having it. She grabs my arm and gives it a tug until I stop. Determined to have my attention, she stands on her tiptoes to invade my personal space.

"You have no idea what you're missing."

Unwilling to mask my displeasure any longer, I move her hand from my arm and take several steps away.

"I won't be finding out. Excuse me."

That wasn't what she expected to hear judging from the pout and disbelief on her face. But I don't have time to care. I round on my heel and continue toward the front door.

"Your loss, asshole."

The words fade into the background as I pick up my pace near the building's exit. I survey the street activity, searching for something, anything to ease the restless energy Alexa inspires. As expected, I spot Cam's food truck among the assemblage of mobile eateries camped out for the noonday lunch rush and decide it's time to get his take on all this. I've been spending lots of time with my old college roommate lately, and though I'd like to say it's because he's expanded his operations to include a new truck near the university, making it more convenient for us to meet up on the days he's working this location, I know better. Cameron Lowell is my confessor, and he'll always give it to me straight. My feet carry me to the truck's window, and it doesn't take long for Cam to spot me. He gestures to his crew to carry on then exits the side door to meet me. We fall into an easy, silent pace as we wander down the campus street.

"So, what's up, man? Where's your girl?"

I look to him and find an expectant, teasing smile.

"What are you talking about, man? She's not mine."

I grind out my reply, surprising myself when I nearly choke on the words. I shift my gaze past him, trying to play it off. When I don't say more, he shakes his head and sighs in that way disappointed parents have.

"Then that's all on you, Roch. How long have we known each other?"

Cam knows things about me that most people don't. We were college roommates when I proposed to my childhood love. After graduation, he kept me from drinking myself into the next dimension when she ripped my heart out and sent it back in a flimsy cardboard box. He watched me let my dick take the lead once I fixed and locked away my heart, and, he's had the pleasure of witnessing the crazy that spills from the obsessive near-stalker I agreed to marry at my uncle's insistence before backing out at the last minute a few years back. Yes, he's my confessor, and if I have any hope of sorting the screams in my head, it's time to lay my worries prostrate at the altar of our friendship.

"She's different from the others. She's a grown up."

This gets the laugh from me that he intends.

"So, what's the problem?"

"No problem. It's just not that deep, I guess." I keep my eyes forward because if I show him that I don't feel any truth in those words, Cam's sure to pick up on the lie.

"If you're going try to shit me and yourself, don't waste my time. Now once again, Roch. Did you fuck it up?"

I give him a rundown of the past few weeks. Cam's seen us together more than a few times but has never asked me about my relationship with Alexa. He didn't have to. He's never seen me socializing with a woman – the same woman – over time. It's been hard to face, but she's necessary. We're a matched set, and it's hard not to want to be around her. Alexa and I click and have since the day we met. Yet, my past and my pessimism hold me back. Cam understands what's behind that and has never tried to judge me for not wanting to let myself be vulnerable again.

Still, I know he's a romantic at heart; he believes in second chances, kindred souls, and hearts and flowers – all the things that give me heart failure. Needing his take, I fill him in on today's texts with Alexa. After some time, he gives me a thoughtful, apprehensive look.

"I've seen you at your best. I've seen you at your worst. Like I said, Roch, this one's different. You're all lit up when you're around her. I've never seen you like that. I can tell she challenges you. Maybe even inspires you. I'd say you've met your match in more ways than one. So, what are you going to do about it, professor?"

I shrug and shake my head. He laughs and I brace myself because he's just getting started.

"Shit, man. You really *are* gone. If it makes you feel any better, it looks like she is, too. So, what's the problem?"

I shake my head again.

"Maybe you're seeing things, Cam. Alexa may have feelings for me, but she says she doesn't plan to do anything about it, and she's shut down. I know I want more than we have, but I don't know what that looks like."

"See, I told you you've met your match."

I consider that as we walk half the next block in silence. What I feel for Alexa makes me uncomfortable. It also fills me with a hope I've never felt before, and that makes me even more uncomfortable and anxious.

"Love isn't something that I know, Roch," Cam says, dragging my internal fight to a temporary halt. "You know that. I grew up without it. And I still haven't found it for myself. But I know it when I see it, or at least see the potential for it, and I've never seen you more at peace with yourself than when you're spending time with her. She lets you be you. When you're with her, you're that goofy, big-hearted hella nerd I got stuck with for a roommate freshman year. And it's nice to have him back."

When our laughter finally dies down, he dives back in.

"You weren't like this with either of your trash exes and certainly not with any of your revenge fucks. You're the only one who can give yourself permission to take a chance on a relationship."

I let his words settle and try to sink in but something inside of me protests at their simplicity.

"Wanting her and keeping her are very different things, Cam."

"For fuck's sake, if you want her, you'll have to work for it because as dazzled as she might be by your good looks, my boy, something's holding her back, too. Find out what it is, but first, know you want the risk and be willing to figure out how to make it stick. I don't think you play around with a woman like that. And I don't know what else to tell you, man."

He stops at the next corner, and I know I'm dismissed. He gives a quick slap to my shoulder and with a nod and smile that he dials back as quickly as it appeared, he heads back the way we came. My thoughts crash around as I consider Cam's words. Like always, he said what I needed to hear. But also, as expected, he picked the scabs of my deepest wounds, and I need time to let those emotions settle, for my mind to slow down and sort through my baggage. I'll always live with the sorrow and the regrets. Doesn't mean I have to hoard the bitterness, too. Maybe. Finally. It's time to keep what I need and burn the rest of that shit for good. I slip my hands into my pockets and take a slow pace back as I give in and begin letting myself feel what my subconscious has known for much longer.

Then, I'm going to need to sort how the hell I could ever let myself become comfortable with any of that again.

Interlude Three

THAT Night

FRIDAY, MARCH 1
    NBC Studios
    Near Capitol Hill, Washington, DC

ALEXA

Fifteen texts.

Seven voice messages.

A raging headache and a mountain of indecision.

For the last 24 hours, Mateo's had me under siege, and there's no end in sight. I stare at the phone in my hand, knowing I need to get to work on Gretchen's show tonight. But my concentration is shit thanks, once again, to the green-eyed god.

Mateo: *Lexi, you'd block me if you weren't willing to talk.*

I smile despite myself and huff out my frustration. As much as I want to, I don't know how to believe in him because his moods are as mercurial as the energy he gives off. I'm instable and in my feelings at the worst possible time as he continues threatening the integrity of the cold war between my mind and my emotions. That won't go away unless I calm the frenzy from longing for something I can't control.

I think that starts with being honest. He's right: I would have blocked him if I wanted to shut him down completely. So, though this feels a lot like walking through an old-growth forest with nothing to light my path, I pick up my phone, press on his last unanswered call, and wait for him to pick up the line.

"So, am I still in the sunken place?" No time for niceties or chit-chat, I see, and I find comfort and reinforcement in his lack of formality.

"Time will tell, but I'm willing to talk, Da Rocha."

He sounds distracted during our brief exchange, so I'm not able to read much from it. I know that I'm bringing my mixed-up energy along for the ride, making my filter an unreliable interpreter of the feelings hiding between the lines of our conversation. Either way, we set a tenuous entente and agree to meet for drinks later today. This could be either the smartest or the riskiest thing I've ever done. But I don't let that extinguish the sparks of excitement popping through my entire body. It seems to be the jolt I need to help sail this workday beyond the horizon and steer my thoughts towards whether I'm up to the challenge of navigating uncharted waters and unwieldy feelings.

I don't allow myself to think too much about seeing Mateo as I make sure I'm satisfied with the final edits and packaging of tonight's show. There was a time when I loved the adrenaline rush that came with incubating and maturing the news stories being broadcast to a million and a half viewers, but these days, it's more of a chore than my choice to do this. The time required to find and anticipate the things most likely to piss off advertisers, sponsors, and any other affiliates chucks a crater into the time I need to be certain we maintain our integrity as a news organization. So, with what time I have left, I move through the pieces with the detached precision of a robot all while tamping down the nerves that have my skin feeling too tight and my heart beating too fast.

A quick glance at my phone reminds me to call Lindy, my BFF, my rock, and my foil. She's due to arrive in town for her bi-weekly homecoming, so I'll need to fill her in on why I'll be late.

Belinda Hopkins is my dearest friend. When she received an offer of associate professorship at the University of Virginia, our alma mater, her son, Luke, who is my god child, stayed behind, moving in with me and my boys. Because we still see each other so often, it feels more like she's moved neighborhoods instead of cities. Anyway, it's fair to say she knows me as well as I've ever allowed anyone to. She has questionable judgment, and I learned long ago that there's no advantage to entrusting your shakier moments and times of need to anyone who makes the same mistakes with deliberation. She must want to live with chaos because not much in her life has gone to plan. In every chapter, she finds the struggle. If it's not there, she creates it. I think that keeps her happy, or maybe it makes her feel more alive, conjuring and riding out emotions so strong they shake the world around her.

Thinking of her exuberance makes me think twice about calling. If I'm already on edge about the evening, inviting her to pile on more angst might not be smart. I settle instead for a text, set the phone aside, and do my best to keep my focus on the work until it's time to leave.

Mateo

I have nearly thirty minutes to spare when I arrive at The Beanery, an artsy hole-in-the-wall bistro in Tysons Corner. It's one of many shops that sit behind the vibrant business and high-end shopping district, so it's suspiciously out of place here. In deep contrast to the upscale, Fortune 500 vibes that ooze from the area, the bustling shops shout hipster and feature an eclectic retail mix: from hand-made jewelry to custom beard-trimming salons. But there could be a three-ring circus behind one of these glass storefronts, and I doubt it would get me to turn my head. I'm not focused on the scenery or the retail mix. My mind is stuck on our evening out.

My resolve reminds me of why I'm done playing games with Alexa, well, mostly anyway. The two of us have a long road ahead, and I can't say with certainty that I know where it will lead. That I'll have to force us both along the way is all I know. I let my mind wonder as I wander along the sidewalk, killing time along with some of my anxiety. I come across a store advertising healthy, natural foods, and it gives me an idea. I enter to have a look around, and it's not long before I find something that reminds me of Alexa. I make my purchase, deciding to take advantage of the free giftbox as a nice finishing touch. I stow the gift in my backpack, sling it back over my left shoulder, and am on my way once more.

I'm still trapped by my thoughts when I see her climbing from her Uber down the block. My chest tightens when our eyes connect, and I think my heart just stopped or skipped a beat or something because it literally hurts. She's stunning in a way that screams she's high maintenance and untouchable, but none of that matters now. I clutch the strap of my backpack as if the action might ground the jolt I just sustained.

I have no idea what she reads in my expression but whatever it is tints her cheeks in that way I'm growing to love, and her usually graceful step falters for the briefest moment. Never breaking our gaze, I pick up my pace and don't stop until we're toe to toe.

I'm not sure what passes through and around us as my mind conjures a reel of potent images, reminding me of what's at stake, the good and bad, the risks and rewards. I can guess she's having a similar fever dream if I'm reading her expression the right way – and I must be as we laugh in unison at our silent emotional groping, each of us keenly aware of the nervous tension bouncing between us. I shake my head and look away, feeling a shyness or uncertainty that's never hit me before. I give myself the benefit of some space as I back away and hold my hand out to her.

"Let's go."

We fall into step easily while my mind trips around from thought to thought. But it's not long before the thick silence that hangs in the space between us feels like an unwelcomed third. I spot an unoccupied bench farther down the walkway and head towards it, gesturing for her to sit before taking a place beside her.

"Something's wrong. Tell me." I eye her intently as she hand-picks whatever it is she's deciding to share with me. She's wringing her hands and torturing herself, so I decide to make the call for her.

"You're nervous. Why?"

She shakes her head before letting a harsh exhale escape her lips.

"Of course, I am, Da Rocha! I have no idea what to expect from you! In case you missed it, I've been trying to get you to talk to me for a few weeks. I've mostly gotten radio silence. *Now* you have something to say?"

I can't help the chuckle that escapes or the hand that advances towards her face as I reach for and playfully but forcefully tug at a strand of her hair that partially covers one eye. Seems this has become a thing with us, this hair pulling when I want her attention, and I'll admit, her reaction is a turn on. I sidle closer on the bench, shifting the air from casual to intimate. I'm determined yet off-center as I manage to keep her gaze and give her my reply.

"Yes, Alexa, I have a lot to say. And I'm guessing you do, too. So, let's grab some drinks, order some food," I suggest, standing and pulling her up with me, "and sort things out."

She freezes, and I'm not sure what to expect as I work to calm the chaos and emotion rushing through my veins.

"Sort things out?" she parrots, cocking her head to the side. "What's to sort out?" She asks, freeing herself from my hold.

I mimic the tilt of her head, bend down, and get in her face. "Not here, love," I say, shaking my head to punctuate my words. "If you want to fight, we can fight. Just not here."

I don't need to say more to convince her because as with every interaction between us, words weren't strictly necessary. My eyes tell her that I'm as flummoxed yet captivated as she is. But hers shutter as she lifts her head, straightens her shoulders, and flashes an enigmatic and serene smile.

"Ok, Da Rocha. Let's see what cha got."

We're settling into our corner booth in a spot tucked into the back of the bistro a few minutes later, and I briefly wonder if coming here was a mistake. Tonight features local artists I see from the stage signage and from the collection of singers and poets buzzing around the bistro's sound system as they check accompaniment tracks, mic levels, and their overall readiness to perform. To the left of the small commotion, a woman paces back and forth, her lips moving as if to ensure her memory is airtight. A couple of guys dressed in colors that could pass for construction zone markers seem impervious to the stares they're attracting as they argue with gusto, hands flying as wildly and colorfully as their attitudes. Despite the seriousness of their preparation, the place feels more like a dress rehearsal than an actual performance. There might be 15 patrons here, and I can't speak to anyone else's plans, but I could pass on the talent show. I need to have this conversation with Alexa. I reach for my backpack and feel around inside until I locate the medium-sized box. I place it on the table and slide it in her direction.

"This is for you."

She looks at it, her curiosity and hesitation colliding, competing for dominance. When she looks at me again, I see that hesitation has the advantage.

"A peace offering, love," I say with a smile that I hope calms what feels like her urge to bolt and never look back. Again. I push the box closer to her and watch as she opens it with deliberation while I fight back the anxiety swimming in my gut. Once she's unboxed my gift, she pulls out the drawstring bag inside and gently releases the ribbons to inspect the contents. She giggles and looks up at me, amusement dancing in her eyes.

"Trail mix?"

"Yes, trail mix," I confirm. "I remember you said you made your own and it was top shelf. There's a shop nearby that sells squirrel food and all that other healthy crap you seem to enjoy, and I wanted to see how this compares with yours. So, cheers, love. Let me know what you think."

She looks struck for a moment before her expression softens and words leave my mind. Her smile is soft, shy even, and it's a chore for my eyes to keep contact with all that I see in hers, so I reach for my water and take a deep drink.

"That's so sweet and thoughtful, Mateo. Didn't know you were listening that closely." She reaches over and gives my hand a gentle squeeze. "Thank you. I'm touched."

Is it hot in here? Heat crawls up my neck, and it's my turn to feel shook. *Da Rocha, you ass, get a clue. Man up.*

"Does this mean you're talking to me again?" This is the easier path to travel, since I know, at least within a range, she'll challenge me, effectively walking us both away from the sentimental plank that keeps daring us to test it.

"Oh no, Da Rocha, that's not on me. You're the one who went silent."

"We both did, Lexi. It's part of the games we play."

"Why do you call me that?"

"Stay on topic, love. One thing at a time," I dodge, but I'll have to remember to quiz her on her issue with the nickname thing later. "We wouldn't need the games if we knew each other better."

"I can't believe you're back to that, Da Rocha! We know each other just fine."

"Nah, Lex. We know shit about each other, only what we let the other see." I lean in closer to breach the emotional distance she's hoping to keep between us. "I don't think you even know what you're running from."

Our waiter picks this moment to show up to collect our orders, and when I look over to Alexa, I see she's not happy with the timing of his arrival either. That feeds my confidence and my impatience with Schuyler, who has the look and feel of a surfer dude. He's a little too west-coast casual about everything, taking his sweet time to chat us – well, Alexa – up as he scribbles our orders. When he can bring himself to stop eye-fucking her long enough to take my order, I let him see my irritation and wait for this idiot to catch a clue. He does, I order, and he leaves almost as quickly as he appeared which is more than fine by me. Small talk passes between us while I wait for the gawking douche to come back with the plate I requested. Once he does, I grab the saltshaker and screw off the cap.

"What are you doing, Da Rocha?"

I smile but shake my head because she'll need to wait. After setting the top aside, I pour the white crystals on the plate and push them around until I have a fairly well-formed line. When I'm satisfied with my work, I meet her curious stare and begin to explain myself.

"Thought I'd be the one to draw the line this time. Maybe that way I can get you to settle down and be real. That way, when I cross it, you won't get so pissed."

I'm not surprised by her frown, but I'm not ready to explain myself either. I have things to say and set in motion.

"I wasn't avoiding you to be a jerk. But I needed to work through some things. I also wanted to get your attention."

"Get my attention? So, you ghost me?"

It takes longer than it should to move her off that, but I find I don't mind as I test my resolve one final time before I go fishing.

"You'll have to forgive me for all of that," I say once she's unloaded what's been canned and fermented in her mind and heart. I feel her bitterness, her longing, her indecision, all beating at my chest, commanding the rhythm of my heart to fall in line with the cadence of hers, which changes, syncopates as she tries to come back to herself.

"You also need to admit I'm right," I push on and hold up a hand to stop whatever disapproval she was about to raise. I don't think she's used to being silenced, but as with so much else between us, discovering the origins of that fun fact will have to take a back seat while I break her down.

"I know you hate your gig. You've got kids. And though you're cagey about the rest, I've figured a few other bits out on my own. Now what can we say about you? You know that I teach and where, we share some views about information consumption, throw a few other random facts in there, but that's about it. And it's not enough."

Her frown encourages me to race through the rest of these words before either of us catches the notion to run away from them.

"Look, Lexi," I push on, needing to take control and steer her thinking. "You refuse to see me. All you see is what you've heard and what you've decided to believe. I believe I can thank Vanucci for that. But what you see doesn't track with that hype, so you don't know what to think. No way you can know what you want when you won't let yourself relax and see me. And that's what we should talk about."

Her laugh doesn't take on its usual lightness and lilting texture. This sound is more like a mad scientist or angry banshee. Not sure which.

"You're out of your rabid-ass mind, Da Rocha," she chokes out, pointing a finger at me. "You have no idea what I—"

"Then, show me I'm wrong, Lex."

Her eyes fill with the familiar fire that lashes out at me when I piss her off. Each time, the fire calls me to walk into the flames, licking and singeing at my need, at my desire to be lost in her. It's not the time for day-tripping, though, so I fight against the urge because I need her open and unguarded. I reach for her hand and link our fingers.

"Let's play a game, love."

"A game? We should be talking, not—"

"Woman, would you stop? We'll get to that. Trust."

I grasp her hand more tightly and watch her until I know she's with me. Her breathing slows, her eyes dilate, and her lips part the slightest bit. That's my cue to continue.

"I don't know where this is heading, you and me, but this isn't a typical friendship. I don't think about my friends the way I think of you. If you didn't feel the same things, you wouldn't be sitting here with me now, not after the past few weeks. So, you owe us the chance to get to know each other without noise drowning out what's real."

The waiter's untimely arrival stalls my momentum, but I don't shoot him too much shade because it'll be good to have my props. I pull my hand from hers as he sets a margarita in front of Alexa and gives me the several tequila shots I ordered with brows raised for approval, backing away when I nod in response.

I place two of the shot glasses about six inches away from my side of the salt line and the remaining two on her side then look up to catch her gaze.

"The game's called Toe the Line." I hold off on sharing my arbitrary rules – in part because I haven't finished making them up – but also because I have more to say before I switch off the emote button.

"You're wrong about me. And you're scared of what you're feeling."

"I'm not wrong, and there's nothing to fear, Mateo. Nothing's going to happen," she answers too quickly, defiance candy coating each of her words.

"We'll see, love. So, see this line?" I ask and point to the salt on the plate. "Think of this as the sexual tension between us. Now that it's out in the open, we can just let it sit for a bit."

She passes a few amused looks between the salt line and me before asking, "Then what are we supposed to do with it?"

"Glad you asked. Then we must toe that line. I'm going to say something I think I know about you that has nothing to do with the stuff we don't want to say. I can walk up to that line, but I won't cross it. And if I do, I have to drink."

"What's the stuff we don't want to say?"

"How about a practice round?" I offer and clear my throat for effect. "This is the stuff we don't want to say." I lean in a little and urge her to do the same. "Your body does insane things to mine."

She drops her eyes, and though I can't be sure in this light, I'd guess her cheeks glow that dusky pink that makes it hard to resist my need to explore a few of those insane things with her right this minute. It's an effort to blank my face of any expression, but I don't think she notices because she's still recovering from my comment.

"Now, here's what I *can* say," I continue. "I think you may be a runner. Am I right?"

"I don't think I want to play your game, Da Rocha," she says, her shaking head an exclamation point to her words. "What will it solve?"

"I'll prove my point and I hope you'll have a new outlook on things between us." I give her no further chance to rebuff me and jump back into the game.

"So, go on, tell me, am I right, about running, I mean?"

The way she looks at me suggests resistance, discomfort, and a little resentment, all of it getting under my skin. I force myself to ignore yet another layer of her defenses and stuff down my own resentment. She nods and gives her reply at last.

"Yes. I like to run."

"It's in the way you move," I respond. "I see strength. I see grace. Determination."

From the look on her face, it's a safe bet that her mind is only now catching up with where this is going, which makes this a great time to reinforce her thoughts.

"You'll see what I did there," I say with a wink and move one of the shot glasses a bit closer to the line of salt. "I walked right up to that line and learned something new and non-sex charged about you at the same time. Now, you go."

She chuckles and shakes her head. "Da Roca, you're a clown."

"Perhaps," I agree, shrugging her off, "but I think clowns are terribly misunderstood and undervalued. Did you know that creativity and ingenuity are important qualities in any clown worth his salt?"

She rolls her eyes and reaches for her margarita. After a healthy drink, she places the glass in front of her and gives me a small smile.

"Do you believe in telepathy?"

I can't read her expression, and her question feels random. She raises her brows in question as I frown and ask her to be more specific.

"Um, sure. Are you clairvoyant?"

"Not at all."

"Well, the way I see it," she explains, "you can read my thoughts. All of them. Even the dirty ones that I wish to keep to myself."

"Nicely done," I say as she raises one of her shot glasses in toast before moving it a step closer to the salt line. "What you may want to keep in mind," I say, urging her with my finger to lean in and meet me once more, "is that I study human behavior, so if you give more of yourself away than you intend, I'll notice. And, so we're clear, our dirty thoughts have been hanging out in the ether together for a little while now."

As we laugh, I think I see the first signs that she's relaxing into this and that I either need to keep her talking or drinking. Never one to find appeal in or much use for drunkenness in anyone, I cast my rod once more.

"You're not always so cautious with men, I don't think. Why with me?"

There. I see I've struck her some place deep, significant, and raw. She recovers from my direct hit with practiced, expected grace, her mask in place once more when she gets up and walks over to my side of the booth. I slide over to accommodate her.

"You and I can't work, Da Rocha," she says with her eyes while her hand reaches over and slinks between my legs, sending an urgent counter signal. "But how about a compromise?"

In answer, I reach down to stop her exploration.

Alexa

I see his slight wince when his hand removes mine. I'm not prepared for the profound sense of loss that I feel, making me surrender what I thought was the emotional upper hand. Desire darkens the gray-green of his eyes as it drags me along at his much slower pace and ensnares me in its unyielding grasp. It takes what seems like days instead of seconds for him to bring my hand to his lips for a kiss, lace our fingers, and return our hands to his thigh.

"That's not toeing the line, love, and that's not what you want either." He places another kiss to my fingertips before breaking our connection. "That's not what this is."

He dials back his desire and lets me see the important parts. He appears sincere. And maybe a little uncertain, too? I'm not sure, but as with all things Mateo, my guard slips at his gentle command, and *my* important parts – the ones I keep sealed tight in a steel vault anyway – are his for the taking. And he does. Take them, that is. The recognition I see in his eyes lets me know I'm right.

"I want to know more of you, not fuck you out of my system," he says, his voice hopeful and determined. "I need to understand the pull between us, and it's not just about sex. Give me – give us – the chance to do that."

I swallow. Hard. This has been his consistent battle cry. Well, mostly anyway. And as my mind catches up with that reality, I can't look away from those damned eyes. He has me cornered. Captured. Completely. Exactly where I want to be.

"And then what?"

"And then. We'll see."

The next half hour passes in such a blur that I put one of my superpowers to good use: emotional detachment. I'm convinced that I can feel the weight and the woes of the world – literally – and to manage my powers of empathy and the hypersensitivity that goes along with that, I do the opposite and detach.

Don't want to be the standard bearer of others' pain and woes? I take my mind out and observe with my emotions walled off and at a safe distance.

In the time it takes for Mateo to defuse my come-on, talk me back around, and convince me to hang out and talk tonight, in fact, *all* night, I've fought to keep my emotional distance even as I've admired his efficiency, determination, and what seems like complete commitment to his information quest. I'm not sure what's more intoxicating: the fact that I'm overcome with my feelings for him, the enchantment I feel at his infatuation with me, or the tequila. I ponder that as he settles the check and pokes around at something on his phone's screen. I take this chance to text Lindy to let her know I won't be home. Her immediate reply demands a call for the details, which will have to wait until morning. I tell her as much and tuck my phone away right about the time Mateo finishes his business and returns his full attentions to me. When he explains that he's confirmed reservations at a nearby hotel, I wonder if he's changed his mind about skipping the deep stuff and letting our bodies do the talking. He dispatches the idea as quickly as I telegraph it, explaining he wanted to find a place where we could be comfortable without being bound by the clock. I let instinct continue to take the lead and agree, equal parts eager and apprehensive to see where the night will take us.

We take a brief Uber ride to his chosen hotel in relative silence, but neither of us feels compelled to fill it this time. He reaches for my hand and rubs gentle circles with his thumb, his touch meant to soothe and to calm. I clasp on a bit tighter as I realize that I've agreed to let him lead us away from the safety of friendship into the maelstrom of our attraction. This is uncharted water, this sharing of thoughts, ideas, and feelings. I let the possibilities wash over me, far from certain whether I'll wash ashore or remain at sea when the morning comes. But instead of feeling panic, I feel like I can breathe again.

I won't worry about the blind corners ahead or the fear that continues to linger just beneath the surface of my skin. Once we've checked in and settled, I take advantage of the liquid confidence afforded me thanks to the bottle of tequila that Mateo somehow managed to finagle from the restaurant as I take this let's-figure-out-if-we-can-have-a-relationship thing for a test drive.

"All right, Dr. Da Rocha. I have a problem with no easy answer, and you may be the only person to help me through this."

The look he shoots me challenges my assertion.

"Don't lay it on too thick, Lex," he chastises through a hearty laugh. His face sobers when he realizes that he laughs alone.

"Something to know about me, Mateo," I say once his look sobers, "is that I've learned it's best to keep my own counsel. That's for lots of reasons. But mostly, it's to do with the fact that trust has never ended well for me. Not with my parents. Not at work. Not with friends. And certainly not with my ex-husband. But I'm looking past that now because I need some help with a huge decision. And because I trust your judgment. Your thoughtfulness. So. Please."

He eyes me with regret, I think, once he acknowledges the trust I'm deciding to place in his care. My smile lets him know he didn't offend, and I lay out this mess.

Earlier today, Sam Stone, a founding partner of Storey|Fischer|Stone, extended an offer to join his firm. That wasn't a surprise given that Sam has been twisting my arm about coming to work for him for months now. Long acquainted with my family, Sam is known for his full-court press, which I know from experience I can't break. I may be able to back him down for a bit, but without speed and some muscle, my defense is no match for his overpowering drive to score. I'm holding him off for now as I think through leaving this career. He wants my answer first thing Monday, and though I thought I was ready to leave broadcast news behind, I'm not sure this is the best fit for me.

Because he's a diligent and practiced listener, Mateo inspires me to overshare. He watches me intently but without judgment from his perch across the room as I tell him my misgivings. I tell him what excites me. And I tell him the biggest truth of all: I'm scared of the challenge.

"Maybe you're scared of the change, but you don't run from challenge."

My brows raise at the suggestion, and I fold my feet beneath me on the sofa while I consider his suggestion.

"But how would you know that if you don't know much about me?"

He walks over to join me on the sofa and points to where I sit. Not sure what he wants, I frown again as he explains.

"Your feet. Give me your feet."

When I unfold myself and do as he asks, he begins a slow, relaxing massage, and for a minute, I'm afraid I may melt at the sensation. Slowly, sensually, and with the intent to seduce, Mateo caresses and kneads at my insteps, the balls of my feet, and my heels. His hands are on my feet, yes, but I feel each stroke, tug, and rub awakening my desire and creating a desperate yearning for more. For him. For more with him. I'm grateful when he jumps back into the discussion so I can try to focus on something other than the wicked magic in his hands.

"You're here, aren't you? In spite of all your misgivings, you haven't run away yet. At least not so far that I can't catch up with you." He tugs on my foot enough to drag me closer then continues to seduce me with this indulgence. "So, I don't think challenge is what's bothering you the most. You like them, and you embrace them."

"Partly right," I say, praying I don't sound as drunk on pleasure to him as I think I might. "This change is a huge risk. To my reputation. Maybe my career."

"Remember what you said a few months ago at Vanucci's vanity fest?"

That makes me laugh. "What's with the two of you?

"Stay on topic, Lex. I want to know if you meant it when you said that someone needed to make a change, to take a lead in rewriting what's accepted as good PR, as standard journalism. You could be that someone in a role like this."

"Oh, Mateo, I don't know. I'm one person."

"Lexi—"

"Ok, stop it with that. Why do you call me that?"

"Tell me why it bothers you."

I shake my head when his eyes implore me to explain myself. But he's having none of my resistance. He pulls me closer still, bringing both of my legs to drape across his lap and my butt a touch away from his thigh. Resigned, I give him the best smile I can muster, lower my head, and launch into the Spark Notes version of this non-story.

"When I was a child, Lexi became Sam Stone's nickname for me. He worked for my, um, my dad, and was often at our home. I was always underfoot, and he said it was like having a little pixie bouncing around. That's when he began calling me that, though it never stuck for anyone else. I remember my ex hated it. He said it was a child's nickname and decided to call me Alli, which *I* hate. I had an aunt by that name who favored my sister and made it clear that I didn't measure up. Didn't matter to Trent, though. It was what he wanted, so it's what he called me."

"Good to know ... Lexi."

I shake my head once more when his wry smile dares me to challenge his determination. I don't and instead melt into the inevitability that at some point, I'll no longer want to continue my resistance campaign. But I don't give the inevitable too much thought, choosing instead to live in this moment of exploration and discovery. We table the Storey|Fischer dilemma and chat our way through the night. I recount thoughts long ago lost to memory and stripped of importance. He shows me that there's more alike about us than is different. More to explore. So, so much more. He even suggests we meet for a run. But I run alone, so I make no promises there.

We fall asleep fully clothed at some point in the early morning hours, side by side on the bed but a safe distance away from tempting fate. When my eyes open to see the new day poised on the horizon, I get up as quietly as I can and make my way towards the en suite. After taking care of business and splashing water on my face, I take a moment to consider my reflection. I feel my cheeks heat (probably because I *am* in heat), so I crack open the door in the hope that better air circulation will calm my mood and nerves. Something changed last night between Mateo and me, the evidence of which stares back at me, mocking me, *daring* me to be honest about what's real. My eyes are too bright, and my heart is finding it hard to remember why listening to my head was a good idea in the first place. *This will never do.*

"What won't do, love?"

I watch Mateo's reflection crowd the door frame as I wish for invisibility. Instead, I meet his eyes and wet my suddenly dry throat with a swallow.

"I, um, I'm feeling—"

Mateo catches my indecisive mood, closes the space between us, and grabs my waist. He urges me around to face him and drops his hands to claim mine. He brings one to his mouth and dusts a kiss across my fingertips.

"Oh no. You're right. That'll never do, love." The gruff edge to his voice cries out to my heart and arrests my attention. "Let me take care of business, and we'll talk in a minute. Wait for me."

I leave him to it and pad across the room to the bed. As I try to calm these nerves and find my center once more, my heartbeat picks up a little as I acknowledge my instinct to bolt out of the door. He was right. I feel like I want, like I *need* to run. *Isn't this what you want? Someone who can feel the desires of your heart and respect them?* I wring my hands in my lap as I roll the notion around in my mind for not nearly long enough before Mateo reappears. His lips curve in that slow, sexy grin that I'm coming to crave, and I resist the urge to pinch myself to test the theory that I must be trapped inside another of my fantastical reveries. Yes, I'm uncertain about what comes next. But for now, I know this one thing: I'm where I want to be. I want to travel this path with him. What I don't know, though, is whether I'll remain intact once we arrive. We're not children, and the weight of the longing between us demands careful handling and nurturing.

I try to clear my face of any of the many tells I know Mateo's worked out over the past months as he kneels before me, spreads my legs wider, and wedges himself in the space he created. With deliberation, he bends to place a kiss on my cheek, and shakes his head as if to admonish.

"Thank you for last night, Lex. But I want you to promise me something, yeah?" I nod on instinct. "The next time you get the urge to run, give me a call. We'll hit the trails together."

His smile disarms me, but I manage to catch the double meaning in his words though I can't form a proper response myself. I can only smile and nod as he closes the space between us, and I don't stop him, can't stop him. The kiss he places on my lips is intoxicating. Promising. It's chaste yet passionate, and I know my heart has at last seceded from my head. I'll no longer wonder what makes him so dangerous. I see clearly now by the way he looks at me, sees through me. It's in the ways he shows me he's as helpless to control what's between us as I am.

I can't process the sensory overload, and I feel my tense shoulders release a little as he pulls away before either of us caves to our lust. It leaves me wanting yet grateful. Confused and consumed. He stands and takes a small step away to break the moment, but that's where my clarity about him begins and ends. All I know now is that this night together has changed everything between us, even as we continue taking careful steps around each other.

Interlude Four

The Carnival's in Town

THURSDAY, JULY 11
 The Offices of Storey|Fischer|Stone
 Tysons Corner, VA

ALEXA

"I think I might hate this gig."

"Shush," Lindy admonishes, her face stern. "Someone might hear you. Besides you're just having a bad day. Happens."

I pour the rage her words unearth into the glare I launch at my phone's screen but distill from my words. "I don't think you get it. I left a stable, successful career for this mosh pit."

By the time I caved and joined Storey|Fisher in March, Sam had me convinced that the firm needed a little organizational restructuring and training before we could begin work on a rebranding strategy. With these hundred plus days under my belt, I question when Sam last spent any significant time around here. Morale is broken. The culture is toxic. The leadership team is a disjointed union of weary pros and once-excellent, high-dollar administrators riding the employment wave to new-client commissions, annual bonuses, and retirement. Our clients, most of them it seems, are beyond redemption. Change won't come to this place without a mammoth battle, and I'm not convinced a win wouldn't be Pyrrhic.

"Don't be dramatic. And don't give up."

"That's right," I say, put off by her simplicity. "Good. Better. Best. Never let it rest!"

"Don't be a bitch either. That's not nice."

"And you're not helping. I don't know what to do." I plead into our FaceTime call with urgency. "I know you always keep it positive, but this is serious. I can't afford to get this wrong. The job I thought I was hired to do? This isn't it. I didn't know the full story. Sam can't know how bad this is. Or if he did, he didn't tell me."

"Hey, look. I know you like things ordered so you know what to expect."

The buzz of my intercom steals my attention. The receptionist announces a delivery, and I ask her to have someone bring it to my office.

"You haven't been there long enough to know whether you like it. Just hang in. Keep learning, and all'll be well. Trust me."

To keep from rolling my eyes at her eternal optimism, I turn toward my door, motion the intern to enter as she approaches, and thank her for the package.

"What's that?" Lindy asks, her excitement bubbly and youthful.

I laugh. "I'd have to open it to know that, wouldn't I?"

"Well, go on! Do it!"

I give in to her childlike happiness and tear away the packaging. Beneath the eco-friendly brown-paper wrap lies a familiar box. I find inside a familiar drawstring bag cushioned on a bed of shredded, crinkled papers. There's a card, also sustainably designed from recycled boxes, attached to the bag with ribbon.

"It's trail mix from one of the local shops." I try to give her a neutral expression as I meet her eyes on the screen once more.

"Who's it from? What's the card say?"

"From a friend. I'll read it later."

I don't know if she'll let me dodge her question, but I'm willing to try and find out.

"Oh, no, ho. None of that. You will tell me this minute!"

It's a whole effort to contain the snark that wants out of me. I don't think I can hide my inner struggle from her if we start talking about Mateo. Again, though, I'll try.

"I told you that I'd met someone. A few months back. He sent it."

"Um hm. This is the one you spent the night with, right?"

"We didn't spend the night together. Not like you're making it sound." I pile the words one atop the other in my desperation to head off this discussion and veer it back toward safe ground. "But yes. Him."

I know I'm screwed as I watch her expression morph from curious to devilish.

"So, he's sending you gifts?"

"It's not a gift."

"Is so!"

"No! It. Isn't!"

Lindy's laugh is hearty, incredulous.

"Damn, girl! Why you playing defense? What's up?"

"Drop it, Lin."

"Nope. Not dropping it." She sits studying me before exclaiming, "You've fallen for him!" Her grin drips with mischief as her glee crawls under my skin, but I dive in anyway. She won't let it go otherwise.

"I have enough going on here at work. Just let me focus on that for now."

"Still can't get out of your way and have some fun, huh?"

"He's not for fun, Lindy," I say, giving this up in hopes that *she'll* give up. *He's for keeps. That means I can't have him.* "He's not for me."

"Seems he thinks differently," she sasses and points to the crunchy treat on my desk.

I wave her off and try to keep my face neutral. "Don't read too much into it. I'm guest lecturing his class this evening. It's a token. A little way to say thanks."

"That doesn't require gifts. He could use his words."

I blow out a breath then take a slow, deep draw of air, hoping to lift my patience along with my endurance for her invasion. "I've told you. Nothing's happening. So, put those thoughts away."

"Keep telling yourself that crap. You might believe it eventually. But I know you. You're torturing yourself over what happens when it goes bad. If the emotional roller coaster you're riding is any clue, I think there's potential for something really stellar, and so do you. "That's why you're running from it."

I hate when she reads me so well, and I'll have to remind her of that one day soon.

"Maybe. Who knows? But I have to go. You got anything else for me?"

Her smile grates as she waves me off. "Nah. Go. Think about what I said. You know I'm right. Be open to new possibilities."

I flip her off, end the call, and reach for the drawstring bag. I turn over the card to find Mateo's message. Simple. Direct.

Thinking of you.—M

I return the gift to my desk, sit back in my chair, and close my eyes. Whether or not he's near me, I feel him. Everywhere. He consumes me. All of me.

Me, too, Mateo. Me, too. Why can't I make it stop?

Mateo

They say you can tell a lot about a man by the company he keeps. This proverbial they, for once, might be on to something.

I've never been the type of man to forge tight relationships, and I can thank my degenerate father for that. Inspiring fear was the glue he used to keep the people around him loyal. Lucky for me my mother was the antidote to my father's tyranny and inhumanity, always encouraging me to embrace instinct and trust intuition. Her words and lessons were my constant compass from the time I arrived in the States, armed with a pocket full of English and a chest load of anxiety. In those days, I trusted no one but craved something familiar. My roommate, Cameron, became that familiar place for me. He was the reasonable meter stick I used to size up people and interactions. As a result, I have countless acquaintances, a business partner I can trust, and two friends. Never one to mass up with people, I keep my friendships separate most of the time.

I might have mentioned that Cam is my confessor. I say what's irritating me; he speaks to the heart of things. Then there's Becket Oliver, another associate professor at the university. His mind is as razor sharp as his wit, which explains his ability to strip the pretense from any situation so you can see what lies beneath it. I don't know why he wastes his time playing professor. Hell, most days, I don't know why I do it. But, as I've said before, I'll leave that to obsess on some other day.

Right now, I'm about to pour gas on my obsession with Alexa. Since the night we spent talking, I've gotten her to calm down and be real. There's always been this easy way between us, but now? It's like the dam can only hold so much longer. We're beginning to know what's real about each other, and that's been good. Other times it feels like we're stumbling through some intricate dance that can't end soon enough, especially when the chemistry between us threatens to combust.

Today, she's guest lecturing another of my classes, but something's different this time. I'm anxious about seeing her as I head down to the building lobby to wait for her. Some careful and targeted online stalking lets me know she's training for a race. It would explain why she's changed our meet-up plans so she could get in more runs, so I guess this is something she's serious about. My mind sticks on this detail as if it'll hold the answer to everything, everywhere. *Maybe I'll figure out why I can't keep myself from this endless pursuit.* Like each time that thought passes, I swipe it away and pick up my pace as I head to the lobby. A few students begin trickling in on their way to afternoon sessions, so I can expect Alexa's arrival soon.

"Someone has his thinking cap on today." The familiar voice catches me off my guard and pries me from my thoughts.

"What's up, Beck?" I answer as casually as I can as we exchange a greeting. I don't want him probing today. He gives me the once-over, so I know he's picked up on my introspection. Lucky for me he doesn't pry.

"No new complaints, man." He shakes his head, but now I know he's the one not being entirely honest.

"Tell you what. I have class in a bit but want to go grab a few after?"

"I'll meet you at Marisol's around 7."

I hear his words and give him a nod and my goodbye, if you can call it that, when I see Alexa and press ahead to meet her. I did say I didn't want to give Beck the reason today, and I so I don't.

Becket

"Matt, man, did you hear me?"

"Seven, man. See you then."

His voice is a mumble as he rushes past me towards a woman who looks like she's been lovestruck when she spots him. He wraps her in a possessive hold that stuns and stops me in place. The greeting itself is nothing over the top, which is surprising based on what I know I saw pass between them. If I had to guess, I'd say it's still early days with these two. I don't have to guess that this woman means something to him the way he cloaks her in his space as they talk. He's marking his territory, and I mark this moment so I can call him on it later. I need to handle an irritant first.

It takes my full strength to keep my head up as I head off to my meeting. This is sure to force my hand to make some career decisions sooner than later, and I feel some type of way about that. Dean Antonio Da Rocha has made career advancement a sport. He's the starting quarterback. The pitcher. The point guard. The rules are his. He's the referee. Many can play. But each time, he must win.

The game I expect we'll play today pits me against his pride. Never one to play at anything with fairness, the dean steamrolls his way to whatever he wants, so hearing from him wasn't a surprise. I knew he'd come for me once he learned I'd left the small academic press that published my first book to self-publish my latest book on generational attitudes towards psychotherapy and personality disorders.

When my first book was adopted as required reading for a few of our psychopathology courses, Dean Da Rocha took notice – and not just in the book itself. He claimed to want to raise our department's profile when he first came to me to arrange for my participation at a university social. What he wanted was a reason to throw a party and be the center of attention. I was the trained seal on display at the dean's petting zoo, his ticket to attention that would never have come his way but for the small slice of notoriety that publishing brought my way. He realizes this. And I suspect today is the day I help him realize that he and his ambitions are much more transparent than he thinks.

He defines himself by and through his role at the university. And though I could do a complete psychological takedown, it's not worth it. In layman's terms, Antonio Da Rocha is an insecure Sigma male. He hates the way the world sees him, so he steps into a persona that makes him seem successful, fearsome, and far more consequential than he is. It's not Imposture Syndrome, though. He's a man who's convinced himself that he's far more capable and deserving than he is. He's delusional, and that's being kind. So, I don't expect I'm going to hear good news at this meeting.

As I near the dean's office, I catch sight of another face I'd prefer to avoid. I can't pretend I didn't see her without causing a scene I'm not prepared to make, and so I keep on my trajectory and arm up for whatever bullshit might come.

"Emery," I greet and hope I've kept my energy neutral, "long time."

As she eyes me from head to toe, it seems to take great effort for her to refrain from turning up her nose. "Oh, Becket," she says, extending her hand from the arm's-length distance she maintains, "what brings you to the admin wing? Shouldn't you be off in class or writing or whatever it is you say you do these days?"

I look at her outstretched hand, to her, then back once more to her hand. My hands remain at my side.

"I have business here, Emery." I give her a nod and try to excuse myself.

"Well, wait now. Before you rush off, I thought it might be nice if we could all get together soon."

I give her my frown even though I know what she's angling for. That doesn't mean I have to play into her hands. She sighs and waves me off.

"Don't be dense, Becket. I mean that you, Amanda, Mateo, and I should plan a date together soon. I'll call you, yeah?"

"Don't bother. That's not happening, Emery."

Amanda Boylan and I are friends with benefits. She's an appropriate companion in social settings, too, but I'd never think of dating her let alone wifing her. She, like her friend Emery here, is a hot, entitled mess with little interest in anything that doesn't bring her attention. She knows the score, but little miss Emery here refuses to use her context clues.

"Emery, don't bother. That ship has sailed." I don't need to tell her that her time with Mateo – out of bed anyway – is long over and done. She must know this. But she won't accept it. Deep-seeded hurt colors her eyes until her shields regenerate and respawn, allowing her to level up to whole-ass bitch mode once more.

"I doubt that, sugar. Bye now." She gives me a wink and sashays off to wherever it is spoiled provost's daughters sashay off to on a Thursday afternoon. I can't be bothered to bother with her, though. I enter the dean's office and brace for what lunacy may come.

AROUND 7 P.M.
Becket

My thoughts are a Cat-5 hurricane.

Unorganized.

Dangerous.

Potentially catastrophic.

I blow through the lobby trying to fight back the rage, my face set in the near-scowl I learned to use when the neighborhood boys used to try me back in the day. My shoulders squared and set in a way that warns off the world, that makes it easier for others to confirm what they've been taught to think about people who look like me.

He's Angry.

He's Dangerous.

Only when I spot Mateo and his woman again do I relax my armor, or I think I do. Even from such a distance away, the mix of passion and caution passing between them is clear for all to see. There's a tense, congested feeling to the scene playing out before me, their longing and lusting worthy of the silver screen. Just as he steps closer to her and leans in, the woman's attention is stolen by something. I'm guessing it's whatever the intruder passing by with friends tosses their way because it causes the woman with Mateo to shrink away from him in haste. Whatever. By now, I've picked up my pace and prepare for the inevitable greeting that'll pass between us.

"And here he is," Mateo says, desperate, I'm guessing, to change the subject. "Becket Oliver, this is Alexa Winston."

She appears both startled and relieved by my appearance and takes a few more steps away from where Mateo insists on crowding her in to offer her hand and a smile that transforms her beauty from remarkable to irresistible. I'm grateful when I manage to remember my manners and return her greeting.

"Sure you won't join us?" Mateo asks her, taking me by surprise with this alien move. Alexa backs away once more, looking panic stricken by the idea. Shaking her head, she declines the offer.

"No, Da Rocha. I told you. The carnival's in town. Another time."

Like the sound of a code word to a spy, her words hit their mark, their directive clear. I watch as my friend goes silent, though his eyes never stray from her. We exchange a few niceties, and I tell Mateo I'll meet him soon, realizing it's time to leave them to it.

Once I'm settled at the bar, I order a double shot of Jameson and a beer to chase it down, which causes the bartender's brows to shoot up. I usually stick with beer, especially on a weeknight, but the past hour has filled me with disbelief and rage. I need to take the edge off before I make a decision I'll regret and let my rage out to set shit straight. I'd be completely justified; after the meeting I endured, I have every right to be an angry black man.

"Damn, Beck! When's the fight?"

Mateo's voice rattles me from my fury, but I can only give him a nod and gesture towards the bar. When he grabs the stool beside me and orders his drink, I note his restless, unsettled, almost boyish affect. When the bartender's gone, he shifts on the bar to face me. This version of the man still hums with energy even as he tries to tame it.

"I don't know that I've ever seen you like this," he says with a slap on the bar. "So, let's hear it then."

I glance at him and sigh. "Just left the dean's office."

My words have the expected effect, sobering Mateo's expression into concern, but he waits for me to say more. I'm sure he reads the clues I give off, but it doesn't take a psychologist to see that I'm agitated. More than that, Mateo takes most situations in stride. It's rare to find him without a smile on his face and something spectacular on his mind. To some, he might seem flighty, dreaming but never achieving. Nothing's farther from truth, though. He dreams big because that's the way he does things – big. His unwavering expression tells me he knows things must not have gone my way.

I push back from the bar and tell him what his uncle told me. "The department strongly recommends that I collaborate with the university's communications office to publish any and all future books I write while employed at American University."

Then, I put the cherry on the dung heap: my tenure might depend on it.

Mateo studies me for a few minutes. "And if I know Antonio, none of this is threats. But he made it clear that he expects you'll make the right decision. Think beyond yourself. Sound about right?"

"That's exactly what he said."

"Yeah, I'm sorry about that, man. He's my mother's brother. But Antonio is an asshole. You'll never hear me say otherwise." Mateo reaches for his drink and downs a healthy gulp. "Tell me what you're planning to do."

I lean over my drink and consider his question. What will I do? I'd been prepared to leave if Antonio found a way to have influence over my work. But "leave and do what?" was the question that needed a solution before I could make that decision with full confidence. An even bigger question now is what's up with my man over here. I know Mateo Da Rocha well, so it's easy to tell something's got him in his feelings. He hasn't cracked a joke. Shows no interest in any of the women vying to be the one he takes home tonight. He's counting on overlooking whatever has him spinning by focusing on me. And we can do that if he wants. But not yet.

"Show me yours and I'll show you mine," I challenge with a smirk.

My arm reaches for a toothpick from the stack placed to my left, and my hand places it between my teeth, which begin to chew. As I focus in to grab his mood or peep a tell, I see nothing. This doesn't surprise me, though. Matt was born a poker player. I'm not supposed to see the truth in his eyes. He also knows I'm assessing him because of course he does. We're psychologists. We play around in each other's minds.

"The hell, Beck?" He shrugs and reaches once more for his drink. He's nearly drained the glass and now I know without doubt he's trying to dull some situation that isn't going his way. He looks away, exhales, and waves me off.

"That's the way you wanna play it then?" I chuckle and prepare to slice and dice my way to the truth. "All right, then, Matt. What's the story with the woman? And check your answer carefully, bruh. I saw you."

He gives a small smile and even smaller shrug, which grabs all my attention. He's looking to ignore it like he does with any weighty issue that comes his way.

"Alexa guest lectured today. Not a big deal, Beck."

When I give him a smile that lets him know I know he's full of shit, he mutters some curse but doubles down on his denial.

"Back off, Beck. I said there's nothing there. She's a friend. That's all."

I let the laugh escape me this time even though it's obvious he's dug in and more than a little irritated. Or maybe determined. Can't tell which. Though I'm willing to cede this round and leave him to his frustration, I'm just getting started.

"Ok, ok. Fair enough," I say, feigning surrender. "Then maybe you're up for hanging out with the lovely Emery. I ran into her—"

"Beck!" Mateo snaps before he realizes his irritation confirms that something about the mystery woman who's in love with him has him off balance. I wonder if he loves her, too. I'll keep that to myself because if I'm right, he's not handling the reality well. Hell, he probably hasn't admitted it to himself. He exhales and attempts to regroup while I sit back, brows raised, enjoying the hell out of my half-cocked buddy. I'm glad for the brief distraction from my own, messy reality, but I doubt he'll let me get away with much more.

"Look," he moves on with a wave that assures me he's shutting down any further conversation about his love life, "I thought we were talking about you. What's your plan, professor?"

As expected. Anytime we hit each other with the honorific, it brings an end to our play time. I don't have to think about my answer, though, because I've been preparing for this possibility.

"Thinking about a sabbatical," I say. "It might buy me some time to figure things out."

"What's to figure out? Submit the paperwork and make it happen."

"For starters, it should be no shock to you that even though I don't love this teaching gig, I like the cash. So, there's that."

I have Mateo's full attention now because truth is, he's not a likely candidate for professor of the year either. We could say we don't like the way the place is run, but that would be too easy. The idea of higher education is fine. In theory. Nurture young minds. Engender curiosity. But in practice, it's more like sitting with a fresh crop of academic squatters year after year, all posing at their basecamp until something more interesting offers them a diverting outcome that holds their attention until the next big thing steals it away.

For me, it's simple facts: I don't like this job. I can't see myself in it for the long haul. Mateo's situation is trickier: How do you convince the dean of your department, who happens to be your uncle, that the career he groomed you for isn't the one you envision for yourself? Or, that he's a douche? Worse yet, I'm not sure Antonio Da Rocha would give two fucks about what another person thinks of him or wishes for himself. That would require a conscience.

"So, do something else for your cash," Mateo suggests, breaking through my thoughts. "You write books. Become a best seller. Problem solved."

I laugh at his matter-of-fact statement. "Just like that, huh?"

"Uh, huh. Just like that." He drains what's left of his drink and summons the bartender for another round for us both, and I let him because it's that kind of night. I side-eye him as I consider his words. *As if becoming a best seller was accessible to all writers at the flip of a switch.* I won't call him on his ignorance, though, preferring this moment of silence between us as we sit staring straight ahead, each of us in our respective, complex network of jumbled thoughts and other people's expectations for what our lives should look like.

"While you're waiting for fame, what do you see yourself doing?"

"I don't know," I say, more to buy time than to gin up an answer. Once I put this out there, aloud, I mean, because I've thought and dreamt of this dozens of times over, I'm not sure it will ever go back into the box where I keep my ideal dreams and deep desires. I swallow to wet my suddenly dry throat before grinding out a reply and letting hope flap its wobbly wings.

"Maybe private practice?"

I know he supports the idea. We've never discussed it, but I know I'm right. It's what else I see that shocks me. He's intrigued and perhaps relieved. *Does he share it, too?* Just when his silence threatens to become odd, he nods his head and hums his assent.

"Practice dedicated to helping men of color—"

"People of color," I correct because mental illness and emotional stress don't respect gender.

"Right, then. Breaking the mindsets that cast generational curses and all that. I like it." He nods again.

I knew he'd get it. Time to see just how much.

"You could be my partner."

Mateo

"I *could* be your partner, Beck. Sign me up and hang the shingle."

I try to sound neutral when I'm anything but. He knows that and isn't bothered. I watch him lean forward and prop himself on the bar, his arms crossed and head down. He's scheming.

Deciding to study psychology hadn't been my choice. Not really. Uncle Antonio agreed to cover my tuition and fees provided I followed in his footsteps. It hadn't been a bad idea at the time. He'd been my idol, my savior from certain hell. So, his path became mine. What I didn't realize was that latching on to Antonio, his sponsorship, and mentorship meant I'd have to become a tenure-chasing minion or lose his support. Back in those days, I was as clueless to the politics of life on campus as I was to Antonio's transformation. Still, I tied my fortunes to his – until I learned he lacked a soul or a conscience.

I've been grateful more than once for being able to read people and situations. I don't play social games; it feels too much like having to audition for a chance to hang with the cool kids, who turn out to be shit humans playing dangerous games with people's lives and futures. My uncle wants to be one of the cool kids, and I'll leave him to all that. It's not for me. I've always kept some distance from this set, being just present enough so I don't raise suspicion with him and his associates. It's getting harder to manage as Antonio keeps at me for more of my time, and that's one of the things that makes Becket's suggestion about private practice a provocative one.

"I'd dedicate my practice to helping children." That grabs his attention. "Maybe see if I can help patch up a few scars. Help fix the things the adults destroy." I clear my throat of the wistful, faraway longing I don't have it in me to explain today. "Never know," I bluster to scrub out any sentimentality remaining in my words. "We might just be the solution the world needs."

When I'm done confirming what he knew and he sees whatever it is he's looking for, he gives a nod and raises his glass. I lift mine, return his nod, and slip back into my thoughts.

It's like looking forward to the carnival. That's it. You remind me of the carnival.

Her words float around my mind, begging for further attention.

"Matt, you with me?"

Beck returns me to my drink, to this place, though some sliver of my mind works to decode the Alexa riddle. I nod and reach to take a sip. Or maybe a gulp.

"You want to talk about it?" Becket offers through snickers and shakes of his head.

"Nothing to talk about." I throw back the rest of my drink.

"Whatever you say, man. Anyway, I wasn't joking earlier. About private practice."

Neither of us is sober, but I recognize when he's earnest. Determined.

"Sounds tempting."

"More than tempting. It's possible. Just. Let's keep talking it out."

I don't know if I'm as brave as Becket. But if I ever were to entertain private practice, I couldn't find a better partner.

"I'm game," I say, giving him my best answer for now. "Now I'm about to head out. Head home."

"Yeah, same. Put this day behind. Start planning what's next."

EARLIER TONIGHT

"It's like looking forward to the carnival. That's it. You remind me of the carnival."

My mind conjures images of public revelry, elaborate celebrations, colorful costumes, and my face tells the story. Alexa shakes her head and explains that she was referring to a carnival of the traveling kind. We share a laugh, and before long, hers morphs into the nervous one that's begun to slip from her when she feels the things she doesn't want to. When we know we fit. When we're in unison. We sync.

"You're like anticipation, Da Rocha," she says. "Waiting. Excitement. But nothing at the carnival goes your way. The games are stacked against you."

I'm clued in to another side of this reality she shares, too. The one her eyes give away even if she won't give me the words. So, I step in closer, crowding her if that's what it takes to extract what I need her to admit.

"Anticipation can be a good thing, Alexa." I'm too invested in what she says and does next and mildly irritated at myself for that. The space between us is weighted with our respective cautions, but I don't back off her. She opened this door, so we're going in.

"I can't go there again."

I see the poorly veiled longing that hides behind the neutral mask she's thrown up as defense. But I can't let her hide this time.

"I think it's too late for that. We're already there."

I don't say more. Neither does she. We're stuck in this moment between us, cemented in place and ensnared by fear and pride. I need to be gentle with her, but beyond what I just said, I don't have more to offer. I don't even know what I'm offering or challenging her to do. Not exactly. I don't think it matters, though, if her eyes are any indication. She seems to recognize my hesitation and lingering confusion as clearly as she sees and feels my desire.

"Careful, honey. That's not how this works."

A chorus of cackles erupts from the tribe of women approaching the place where we stand. I find a satisfied smirk on the face of the one in the center of the pack, the same one I brushed off a few months back when she'd made herself available.

"Private conversation. Keep moving."

I grind out the words then dial back the rage she unearthed. Packed with revenge and malice, the words hit different than when I tossed them her way. By leaving them behind for Alexa to pick up, I'm guessing she's calling this her get back. And Alexa *has* picked them up. She takes a step backward, away from me and from any chance of resolving our standoff. I close the space again and reach for her shoulders to speak for her ears only.

"Don't. You know that's not what this is."

She shakes her head. "*This* is why I can't, Mateo. I can't."

"Stop. Let's talk. I'm meeting a friend for drinks in a few minutes. You can come with us. Give us a chance to talk."

"No, not a good idea." She's firm in her refusal, so when I spot Becket, I decide to try stalling her out to buy myself some time to reroute her doubts.

"He's here now. Becket Oliver, meet Alexa Winston."

Relieved, I think, for the interruption, she steps away from me to say hello.

"Sure you won't join us?" I ask her, not willing to let her off the hook for the evening. I catch her off guard, but she regains her footing and steps away from me. Again.

"No, Da Rocha. I told you. The carnival's in town. Another time."

Though I'm quiet by nature, I'm never speechless. Until now. The hint of bite in her voice and the plea I see in her eyes tell me not to push, so instead I turn to pop a question Beck's way, thinking that might give me some time to find a response to this latest obstacle she's wedged between us. I'm sure he's picked up on the static in the air. I can also tell that his mind's not here, and he's anxious to be off.

I'VE BEEN REPLAYING this scene between us as if I'll find new meaning if I go over it enough times. Without the interruption, without someone there to reinstate the doubt she likes to toss up as her defense for keeping her distance, she'd have relented. I know this. The part I can't figure out is that bit about the carnival.

The laugh that escapes me sounds bitter, incredulous. And I guess I could own those reactions if I thought I had a right to them. But I don't. Alexa's fears played out in front of us, and I couldn't do a damned thing about it. I can't change what happened before her. But I can sure as shit get pissed that she won't see past it. I don't know how far this will get me, but I reach for my phone and open the messaging app.

Me: Hey.

It's not too late, I note on the phone, which reads 8:30. I'm not sure what she's up to, and when I see the text bubbles pop in response, it stokes my hope that she won't blow me off.

Alexa: Hi. What's up?

Me: Trying to work out that thing about the carnival so I understand how to get past your latest roadblock.

There. Short. Direct.

Alexa: I told you. You represent danger. It's smart to run from danger. ☺

Me: (sigh) C'mon, Lexi. For real? Try again.

Alexa: It's too much for tonight. Can we talk about it tomorrow?

Too tired to take on another deep-sea dive, I agree and after a little more back and forth between us, we say goodnight, and I set the phone aside. Weary now, I head to the bar in my living room for a drink of something dark and strong before navigating on heavy legs to my bedroom. Once I'm settled in a chair, I let the regrets I've been trying to silence all day fill the space I'd rather keep quiet. Like the habit it's become, my curiosity about the things Alexa keeps to herself takes over. They're the secrets to her resistance. The keys that unlock the stories behind the version of herself she presents to the world. More and more, she lets me see something else, too. Something more soulful. More vulnerable. Wild. It's the place that connects us, that compels us. It confounds us, too.

I put my heart away long ago, but that didn't keep Alexa from finding it. She's the only one who's been able to. I reach for my glass to chase away that thought along with the residual fear and doubt it leaves behind. On one hand, I'm more determined than ever to break her down. But when I consider what I feel for her and the vulnerability I'd have to expose along the way to have any sort of meaningful relationship, I retreat to the known comfort of hiding inside old habits, cloaking the truth inside the nonchalance that's getting harder to manufacture with her. I stare at my drink as if it holds the answers, but I know better than that.

I know what I want. I just don't know what I'll do with it once it's mine.

Interlude Five

Undone

FRIDAY, AUGUST 2
   One Loudoun Carnival at Uptown
   Ashburn, VA

ALEXA

Still hours away from setting, the sun shines its bright, oppressive, mid-July rays on the sea of people waiting to make this semi-annual pilgrimage to the asphalt paradise known as the One Loudoun Carnival. Replete with the usual rides, unwinnable games, sugary foods, and fried treats, the attraction draws people of all ages and circumstance.

You'd think my sons were experiencing this place for the first time judging from their rapid-fire chatting and nervous, bouncy energy. I pay closer attention to the words passing between them as they complain about the slow pace of the line, and something grabs my curiosity.

"What's the rush, gentlemen?" I ask, startled faces and guilty smirks confirming my intuition. Tristan, my oldest, clears his throat and eyes his brothers, causing them to fall into whatever pre-approved formation they've agreed to assume when they're up to something. Satisfied with what he sees, he gives me his attention.

"No rush, Mom, but this line is taking forever, and we're old enough to be here on our own. You could always drop us. Go do something nice for yourself for a change."

I might have agreed without question if Treat, the youngest of my trio, had managed to control his tell. The restless shifting from foot to foot, his guilt reflex, rarely failed to telegraph when he was plotting or embroiled in the creation of one. I look to him then back to Tristan.

"That's sweet. But that's not all. Go on." I keep my smile bright and encouraging, but just as I know these children, they know this is my signal to consider with great care their next words. Tristan squares his shoulders, but his eyes seem far less certain than his stance suggests.

"Mom, well, I might meet up with some friends, um, *a* friend, I haven't seen since school ended. Well, she's my friend. But she'll be here with her friends, too. So, it's not like—"

"A date," his brothers say in unison, high fiving each other and drawing a promise of certain, painful death from Tristan if the look he shoots their way is an accurate gauge.

"Stop," I say, laughing at the younger boys' shenanigans. I feel a pang of guilt when I see the mild embarrassment in Tristan's cheeks. His olive coloring hides much of what I expect is more like a crimson blush, and his eyes plea for mercy.

"You two stop teasing. And Tris? Is this Hayden?" It takes a death-ray stare from me to convince Treat and Trace to end their comic relief, and that relaxes Tristan a bit.

"Yes. We've been texting and stuff this summer. We just thought it would be cool to hang out."

"I get it. She's a cool girl," I cosign, "but next time you make plans to meet up with somebody, be upfront with me. Easy."

Tristan stands still as I give him WTF hands, his expression unreadable for a moment until the realization hits that he's gotten his wish. I point towards the front of the line to urge them ahead. He mouths a "thank you" before rustling his brothers back into his control. I pay their admission, and we plan to meet in a few hours. I watch briefly as they run down the causeway, disappearing into the dense groups of children, their parents, and, in many cases, *their* parents.

Found time is a luxury, so I'd be wise to do something fun with this slice of freedom. My mind wants to float to the place it always goes these days, but I need to put Mateo away for at least a bit. I stop and turn back to the attractions before me and smile. I spent spring breaks when I was a little girl with relatives who lived in a town called Chesapeake, Virginia, a corner of the state tucked between Virginia Beach and the Outer Banks of North Carolina. A tiny carnival would come to town in those days and set up in the parking lot of the G.E.X. Department Store, which was down the street from my aunt's home. Each year, without fail, one of the parents in her neighborhood would go door to door inviting as many of us kids as he could pile into his conversion van and haul us up to the carnival to be bled of our little money by any means necessary.

It was a great time. Until it wasn't.

One year, I ate myself sick with funnel cakes.

The next, I placed the flimsy little pink rabbit I won shooting at ducks on the side of the game's counter long enough to tie my shoe. When I stood up, it was gone. The carnie running the game told me to keep a better eye on my things and refused to give it back, returning it to the display.

The great Ferris wheel caper was the final straw. My friends and I were stuck at a point around 75 degrees in the air. There we swung for what seemed like a lifetime. At ten years old, my fears wouldn't permit me to appreciate the view of the ground beneath because the height alone captured my awareness and powered my panic. It didn't help matters that I had to watch helplessly as the swaying seats shook free all the money I'd stowed in my pockets. I watched helplessly as the coins poured out like salt streaming from a shaker. By the time we reached the ground again, I was convinced the ride existed solely to separate us from our money so the workers could collect it each evening. And with that, I declared the carnival dead to me.

I can't let go of my fascination with Mateo as handily.

I turn to pace back to my car and begin considering the past few weeks. *You remind me of the carnival.* It's a fun time until something goes wrong or the hurt and heartache blindside you. I'd stumbled through these thoughts for him, wishing I could stuff them back inside my ridiculous mind. What I'd hoped to explain is how he triggers a riot of emotions that overwhelm and ensnare me. I'm held captive by his effect on me, to the idea of what we could have together. But I'm not sure I can open up the bruised parts of myself enough to go all in. All Mateo seemed to hear was another excuse, and he let me know what he thought about it. We've never had harsh words for each other, but my comments brought us as close as I'd like to come.

I know I can't keep up this back and forth with him. It's not fair to either of us. I drag open the door to my SUV, more questions than answers filling my head and my heart. So, I decide to see if I can find a few answers to quiet the back and forth. I sit my purse in the passenger's seat and rummage through until I find my phone. I see that I've missed a couple of messages from Lindy when I unlock the screen, but she can wait. I'm on a mission. I think. I could opt for a text, but something compels me to dial the number instead and have this talk in real time. The phone rings once, twice, and then twice again before sending me to voice mail. My heart flips a bit at the heavy disappointment that takes a seat in the pit of my stomach, but I try not to let it bleed into my voice as I leave a quick message. Just reaching out, I say, telling Mateo I'll try him again later, knowing that's probably not going to happen. Knowing that I'm being silly. It's Friday evening. It's not like we had plans or anything, so I have no right to feel this pang of sadness at not being able to connect.

My brain refuses to be shut down and tries to obsess, but I fight the compulsion by busying my thoughts with my phone. I check my texts and see Lindy's missive.

Lindy: *You free? Phaedra needs some support. Hit me if you're free.*

The message is time stamped about 20 minutes ago, so I thumb my reply, letting her know that I have some time now that the boys have uninvited me to their pre-planned evening out. I receive Lindy's reply almost immediately directing me to Bar Taco. I tell her I'll see them in ten minutes and begin the short drive to the destination.

I've known Phaedra Sheppard for a few years now. She leads a complex life that makes you want to clutch your pearls at times, but she's one of the most compassionate people I've ever known. Lindy introduced us a few years back, and though I like and appreciate her boldness, the two of us can be combustible when together. By contrast, she and Lindy share an easy rapport, but I won't let relationship dynamics spoil our time out this evening. I need the distraction of focusing on someone else's drama for a few hours. Once Lindy explains what Phaedra's facing, there's no more hesitancy, doubt, or delay. My issues will wait.

"MOM, THAT WAS GREAT, but can we go to a real amusement park tomorrow?"

"Yeah! Let's go to Busch Gardens!"

Treat and Trace hit me with their pitch the minute their butts hit the seat of the SUV. Just as quickly, I shut them down with a promise to plan that excursion some other time. I'm met with some groaning and grumbling until I explain that I'll be taking a quick daytrip with Lindy and Phaedra tomorrow, so they'll need to get along without me. I answer a few rapid-fire questions until the boys' attention is exhausted and directed away from me.

Once back at home, I give them my standard warnings about things to do and not do while I'm away. It's wasted effort as they tune me out and peel off to find other diversions the minute they're able. I leave them to it and head to my den. I drop onto the love seat, and as the soft cushions absorb the rough edges around my emotions, I begin letting the thoughts of the day wash over me. Satisfaction can be a tricky state to maintain. I thought I was perfectly happy with my comfortable, still life. I do what I want, when I want (for the most part), in the ways that I want, and that suits me fine. I don't have to confer with another before making the most basic of decisions. I no longer run the group-think gauntlet because *I* am the captain of my fate.

If I'm fine with all of this, why don't I feel fine?

I grab for my phone to check yet again and see a missed call from Mateo. There's no voice message, which is a bit out of character. Before I can talk myself out of it, I scroll to his contact information and return the call. Muffled sounds pour through the connection as he opens the line.

"I'm at an event I couldn't miss. What's up?"

"I, well," I hesitate a moment, put off by the clipped edge to his voice, "I had some free time and thought I might see you. That maybe we could see each other." My words don't sound as convicted in the wild as they did in my head, but I manage to power through and explain my unexpected free time after dropping the kids at the carnival as my reason for the last-minute call.

"Does this mean you're giving the carnival another chance?"

Our laughs tangle, and I don't miss the intentional double meaning behind the words. Neither do I catch what he says next as the background noise ratchets up.

"Can I have you tomorrow?" He repeats, this time in Spanish.

Interesting phrasing, I think as a smile lights my face and moves my mood from skeptical to playful. It's curious that he's flipped languages. It's something he does rarely. Judging from the voices and music clouding the clarity of our connection, I'm guessing it's his way of keeping our conversation private, which is fine. It's the universe of possible reasons why that makes me uneasy. I try to push past the doubts that my self-doubt conjures and decline as I explain tomorrow's last-minute road trip.

One of the things people of color don't, sometimes can't, or perhaps refuse or neglect to plan for is their golden years. It's why many adult children like Phaedra inherit the need to make difficult, life-altering decisions regarding elder care. She has no siblings, and her mother passed away a few years back, making her her father's sole lifeline. I've never met him, but Phaedra's self-torment around this upcoming trip gives a solid clue to the dread that goes along with folding him into her household until she can find a proper living arrangement.

"How long will you be there?"

"It's just a day trip. It's a simple pick up, and we'll be on our way. We're just moral support, I think."

"I'll see you soon then. We have unfinished business."

"Yeah?"

"Yes, Lexi. Safe travels, love."

PHAEDRA

"The Lord doesn't want me, and the Devil won't have me."

It doesn't surprise me that these are the first words that fly from the mouth of the man who consorted to give me life. George Washington Cooper sits motionless, his eyes filled with devilment, as Lindy, Alexa, and I walk the length of the sidewalk to the front porch steps where he sits. I hope I remember to keep my tone and attitude light and positive.

I hope. But I'm not confident.

"Hey, Pops," I say as I find a smile to lighten the vibe.

"'bout time," he murmurs, without greeting me, of course, because, well, there's not much between us. Mom bridged the gap until her passing three years ago. That's when Pops began his decline. His health, his mind, and his tolerance of anything other than what he wanted when he wanted it all took a nosedive as diabetes and dementia began claiming his life in slow, painful steps. Packing up and leaving his home of more than 50 years to come stay with me, the daughter he barely knows and doesn't tolerate – isn't what he wants. In no way. But I'm all he has.

"Time was elders were respected and revered. Not forced to go live with people who think their shit don't stink."

He rakes his eyes across the three of us, settling on Alexa for so long it makes *me* uncomfortable. This lets me know to brace for whatever he says next; even though Pops may be struggling to keep his mind on task, he has no problem finding and acting on his dirty thoughts and still-active libido.

"What's up, sweet thang," he drawls and eyes Alexa like she's his next meal.

"Keep your mouth shut and your pants zipped, old man." My glare meets his sly grin, which blooms into a lecherous, challenging smile.

"You don't tell me what to do, young girl."

Alexa glances over to me and smiles as she takes a step closer and extends her hand to Pops. "My name's Alexa, Mr. Cooper, and it's nice to meet you."

He accepts it and tugs her towards him. On instinct, Lindy and I grab an arm each and lever her away and out of his reach. I lean down to get in his face.

"Listen to me, Coop." My voice is low like the one my mom used with me in church when I was more into playing with my friends on the pew than in praising and worshipping. "These are my friends. *I* know you're nasty, but they don't need to see the show. You're gonna behave, or do I need to go next door and tell Miss Myra we'll be needing her to watch out for you till we can find you a bed somewhere?"

For Pops, the words *find you a bed somewhere* are like kryptonite to Superman. He's made his disdain for nursing homes known for as long as I can remember. Over the years, he let it be known, loudly, proudly, that he plans to haunt me from the afterlife if I make such a move. As expected, then, my words, combined with my use of the familiar nick name, sap the strength from his fight. He falls in line, and the girls and I tell him to wait while we grab his bags from the foyer and begin loading them in my SUV. A truckload carrying what's left of his life is en route to my house, but I'll worry about what remains inside here another time. I need to use these next several hours on the road to figure out what comes next. Pops and my husband, Stephan, can co-exist for short stints, but I need to smooth Pops and his attitude out some in case this temporary stay gets extended.

When we secure the last of his belongings and shut down the house, he asks us to leave him be. As I'm settling in the driver's seat and my eyes look up to meet his, I freeze. It's the first time I've seen him cry.

I'D HOPED THE RHYTHM of the tires on the road would send him to sleep, but I wouldn't have such luck. Not at first anyway. Pops made the first of four hours on the road uncomfortable with his sniping, farting, and consistent complaints about my driving. Then it was complaints about the temperature. After that, he started in on the traffic around us. I take a quick glance at the passenger's seat and toss up a silent prayer of thanks in appreciation for the soft, constant snore that's replaced Pops' grizzled grousing.

"Is this your life now, Phae?" Lindy keeps her tone light and teasing, but I hear the urgent question wrapped within. I find her sympathetic eyes in the rear view and have to look away before they trigger the tears threatening to spill from mine. I shrug and force my eyes to lock on the road ahead of us.

"This'll be easy, Lin, honey. I got him. I got this."

But I don't got him, and I don't got this. Not really. I know moving Pops in puts Stephan and me back on a collision course. We've traveled through the toughest of times before, so the challenge isn't the part that bothers me. The hard truth is that we don't connect anymore. I've decided it's why we don't know how to find our way off the continuous loop that shines light on the lowest points in our life together. After watching this low-light reel *ad infinitum*, you leave the course wrecked, damaged, and defeated. These days, the passion between us flows through a finer sieve, distilling the sharp pieces of our relationship, the ones that left scars that will never heal along with the pieces of our hearts that will never mend. Steph enjoys playing with these daggers, and I expect Pops' arrival to inspire a few rounds of emotional knife play. He's supported the move – even encouraged it – so far, and, as of now, we're clear that bringing Pops to us is a stopgap. Still, I know his agreeing to this will cost me something. I also know it'll be a while before the riddle is solved.

"Phae, what's going to happen during the day? Do you have someone lined up to help you?" Alexa's question is quiet, urgent, near reverent. As I learned while supporting my mom during her last days, resourcefulness, planning, and networking are the one-two-three punch required for success when you enter the elder care ring as primary caregiver. In this corner, weighing more than one would ever hope to imagine or consider, are the bushels of rules, limitations, and hidden exceptions you need to understand to navigate the Medicare machine with success. I stand in the opposite corner, bare-knuckled, alone, but much smarter about what will come with this perpetually uphill challenge this time.

"To start, anyway," I answer. "I joined a Facebook group called Working Daughter. It's a support community for adult caregivers, and I've found some great resources there. People seem to share thoughtful advice as well as their experiences. It's how I found the home health nurse who starts on Monday, so fingers crossed."

Alexa hums her reply, and through the rearview, I see her exchange a worried look with Lindy.

"Oh, no. Just. No. What's that look for?" I'm sure I sound more forceful than I'd like, but I won't be second guessed when I'm the only one working to find solutions. "That look you two keep giving each other. What's that about?"

"Phae, I just think you're in too deep." Lindy's eyes shift from me to where Pops sits in the passenger seat. "He's a lot, not to mention the fact that I've never heard a good story from anyone when it comes to taking your parents in. Are you sure—"

"This isn't permanent," I cut through her words, which I don't want to hear now or ever. I don't want to consider how true they might be. "It's just a stop on the journey to his final destination."

The words are eerily, literally the truth. Where we move Pops will be where he spends his last days.

"And he knows this, yeah? That he's not staying with you till then." I hear the hesitancy in Alexa's voice, which doesn't help my mood. I learned a long time ago never to believe that I'm right about what's in another's head until they confirm it with their mouth. I conjure Steph's Colgate smile to remind me of the sting that goes along with that precious mistake then come up with the proof the girls need to see to know that I know what I'm doing.

"He knows. And we'll all be fine."

So much remains undone and undetermined. How well will Pops adjust to having someone, to having *me* care for him? How will I juggle work and these new responsibilities at home? It's been a long time since I had to worry about balance. Since there was anything other than us to worry about. So, so long. But I don't dwell on that. I can't afford to.

Alexa

It's painful to watch Mr. Cooper as he awakes to find we've arrived at Phaedra's. We all rush from the vehicle to help, but he refuses the helping hands outstretched and poised to assist him as he sits staring up at the house, his eyes dead, his body stiff. Once he gathers himself and leaves the truck, he takes deliberate steps towards the mass of boxes and furniture where Stephan stands. I don't have to hear the words they pass to know this won't be an easy time for Phaedra. After their tense exchange, the older man barely breaks his stride as he passes through the door, into the kitchen, and beyond our sights.

The air around Stephan is always thick, that much more so today. When he turns from his father-in-law to find Phaedra approaching, he squares his shoulders, and I can feel the weight of the complex of emotions that they both must be processing. I feel for Phaedra. There's no way she can't resent having her life changed so fundamentally. From the brief time I had with her father, I can't see him being interested in doing anything to make her life easier. I know she knows that. What comes next is the wildcard. I don't pretend to understand her marriage. It's an open relationship, yet they seem to operate as a unit. A couple. What I see right now are two people in crisis. Two people on two different pages who don't seem eager to bring themselves back to why the hell they breathe the same air. Share the same space. I recognize that place where you no longer miss the past you thought you had. You long for a future you're too afraid to put into play. I can't make out what Phaedra says, but Stephan's response is clear.

"Just keep the old man in line. That's what I need you to do."

Though clipped, the words echo through the garage and carry towards us where we stand on the driveway. He didn't need to say anything more. We all feel his disapproval as he spins on his heel, without ever acknowledging Lindy or me, to head back into the house, giving the door a definitive slam.

LATER THAT EVENING

I shut off the taps to my bathtub, pin up my hair, and climb into the almost-too-hot water swirling around in the soaking tub. From the moment I settle into the sudsy warmth, the day's tensions begin to melt away. Grateful, I fall back, close my eyes, and relax at last as calm begins to replace chaos.

I went for a run a couple of hours ago to release some of the tense energy I'd bottled up throughout the day, so I'm happily exhausted. The several pings I hear on my phone let me know that the running accountability check I started a few weeks back is working. I have no idea how to train for a race, so it's great to get some feedback and encouragement about my progress. Admittedly, most of the moral support is from friends and family, so I decided to step it up and join a local running club. I posted my intention just a bit ago, so I guess my peanut gallery approves.

I open my Peacock app and select an episode of *Charmed* to watch as I enjoy my bath. I find a familiar favorite episode and watch as the witches fight off demons, protect the greater good, and manage to leave enough time to navigate – and resolve – complicated relationship issues. I give in to the temptation to wish. To dream. The eyes that come into focus coax and ensnare me, and for a quick, foolish moment, I wish for a sign such as the one Phoebe's receiving now, the one that lets her know that she finally can trust that her heart's desire is her true love. Unlike my silly witch-show obsession, real life doesn't offer encounters with magical beings imbued with the power to portend our futures. So, absent my own personal Cupid, I need to stand up and do or do not. Easy to say.

I'm not sure how long I linger in the tub, but if the fact that the series finale nears its end as I prepare at last to climb out, my mind's been shut down for much of the past hour. Leo's been returned to Piper. Phoebe and Coop can be together. Henry and Paige sail off into the sunset. And they all lived happily ever after.

"What bullshit," I grumble as I pull myself out of the tub and reach for a towel to wick the moisture from my skin. Of course, that's the precise moment when a familiar ring tone breaks through my thoughts, and I reach for my Air Pods.

"Da Rocha, what's going on?"

"Wanted to see about the trip. How was it?"

I give him the debrief and wish once more for some sight beyond sight. This is what I want. He's what I want. So. *What am I waiting for?*

We bounce back and forth, around and around as I pull on a shirt and shorts and settle into my den for the evening. He asks to see me. But for some reason, I freeze. Heart says say yes. Head intervenes and sends words to mouth that offer my training as an excuse to put him off till some other time, so we say goodnight. Again.

"Be sure to get your rest then, love. Talk soon."

Mateo

I close the registration widget as I listen to Alexa find new reasons to keep her distance. For the first time, though, I'm not frustrated by it. She's thrown herself and all her energy into training for this race, so I'll meet her where she is. Literally.

Thank you for joining the Renegade Running Club. We can't wait to see you on the trails!

I save a PDF of the confirmation to my laptop and consider my gambit. Alexa's hit a wall regarding our relationship. I get it, but I won't accept it. Instead, I'll play things her way inside her world. Within her rules. For now, anyway.

She can keep running. And I'll be right there by her side.

A Coda from Truth

"HONESTLY, TRUTH," HONESTY pleads with me and with some urgency, "I think you need a new game plan."

I eye my sister and consider her prompt. Honesty is temperate, ever the soul of grace and poise. Calm of spirit. Gentle of heart. She's as wise as she is virtuous. And she needs me to take her seriously. I nod for her to say the things that weight her heart and contort her face into the sober, hardened visage I've learned to heed and hear with my heart.

"The world of men has lost its appetite for playing by the rules, Truth. Your sitting around waiting for happily ever after to prevail is a huge miscalculation. You need a few chess moves of your own, sister."

I hate moments like this, those times when I stare down these grand gashes in the societal fabric. Authority is upstaged more times than not by some back-room deal or a secret passageway to an unfated outcome. Yes, I said unfated. I'll need to speak with those dears who document the language because this might be one for the books. The incessant circumventing of rules, regulations, guidelines, societal norms (the list is endless) threatens the world, knocking the natural order of things off its axis. Few recognize me now. And when they do, I'm as welcome as Grizabella the Glamour Cat. I, too, remember the time I knew what happiness was. No one was perfect nor were they expected to be. People made mistakes, lied, cheated, and at some point, often, they atoned. Truth prevailed. They were set free. Lessons were learned. They grew more thoughtful.

Having learned the art of the deal since those salad days, the world finds darker alternatives to integrity on the menu of behaviors that society will accept. Authenticity, too, has lost favor thanks to the rise of Entitlement and Inadequacy. I may not like it, but it is what's true.

"You're playing by a different set of rules," Honesty goes on, breaking me from my thoughts. "A set of rules that fell out of vogue right around the time you got wise to Keats." She knows better than to poke around at that sore spot.

Not one of my prouder moments. But what can I say? Any girl would soften to the notion that she inspired great and timeless poetry. No matter, though. I sit like the stoic that I am and give her this airtime. "You need to come out of the shadows and up your game. You need to knock some heads before you can set things to right for good."

Influence is playing the long game with Mateo, Alexa, and her family. Despite my best efforts to shield them from her whispers, she's chipping at some crack in their foundation, and I'll need to figure out what that is. This isn't about what's real and in front of you. It's about the things you can't see and control. It's about outsmarting illusion. I'd wager her strategy is to distract or reroute me. But Influence has many arrows in her quiver. Powered by Inadequacy and Entitlement, she gains her power by preying on weakness. Humans never were perfect, making them the perfect vessel for her seduction. She creeps through the crevices where self-doubt lives, planting seeds of deception and weaving masks to obscure the true self. The look of people and things supplants and twists reality to benefit even those for whom no benefit is deserved. Fairness is tossed away. Tricks become standard issue in the lives she infects. I can have no effect if I challenge her within my system of beliefs. I know this. And so, I know what I must do next.

"It is not in my nature to game the system," I say at last, turning to face Honesty. "But for this, sister, you are correct. I'll need to step out of character."

My words arrest my sisters as expected. Authenticity bolts up from her disconnected bubble to shoot me her look of horror, perhaps of warning, as she bristles at what I suggest.

"I don't think you're well, Truth," Authenticity says, her voice a mix of hesitation and suspicion. "You can't be something you're not. You should know better than to play with attributes you can't sustain."

I smile at her, my resolve strong and conviction flaming bright thanks to her doubt. "Oh, I'll never lose or forget my authenticity, sisters," I say with amusement and a wink as I pass an arrogant look between them for good measure. "Try to think of it as if I'm simply de-roling. I've played this part my entire life. Time to take a small hiatus from it. Try on something new. Something a little out of the ordinary. Just long enough to shore up cracks and set things back on course. You do remember what I said about that, yes? It may not run smooth."

So, it's time for me to re-route the GPS and shine a brighter light on the lies so we can find our way towards redemption and resolution at last. Patience, loves. Just sit back, relax, and watch me work.

MATEO AND ALEXA'S STORY begins in *Masked Intent: A Modern-Day Morality Play* and concludes in *Intents + Purposes: The Final Act*, which publishes in late 2023.

An Excerpt from Masked Intent: A Modern-Day Morality Play

Prologue

ON THE PLAYLIST OF little-girl dreams, finding happily ever after with your heart's desire is sure to wind up on your Spotify Repeat Rewind set. We make it our goal to make these dreams a reality, and with starry-eyed innocence, we chart our course for the future in search of someone who'll stay constant and be by our side even when the winds shift. Our love will be genuine and tell it like it is.

I could continue to buy into this fairy tale, or I could wake up and face reality. It's been awhile since I've found hope out there, let alone a strong, solid relationship. Time after time, I find myself in bed with the same mix of lies, deception, and maneuvers, all disrespecting and disregarding me for sport, for no reason other than because it suits them and their interests. They think they can dominate and overpower me, and it's all because of *her*.

Before we get to all of that, I should introduce myself. I've been called beauty. I've been called terrible. Some say I'm what satisfies the soul. Still others say I can set you free.

For those of you still riddling your way through all of this, I am Truth, as in *the* Truth.

I'm not sure you've heard about me considering all the chatter about *her* – about Influence. She thinks she can floss and gloss her way through life, rewriting what's been predetermined to her satisfaction, never knowing or accepting Accountability. This *is*, of course, nonsense. I don't have replacement players. There's *only* me.

I've watched Influence seduce so many into doing, saying, or believing most anything imaginable, no matter how heartbreaking, outrageous, or illogical. I simply can't believe the things she gets away with. She's real shiny, that one, and she's almost made me doubt myself a time or two. It's sad to see, but somewhere along the way, flash replaced fidelity as the standard of excellence. Never mind the consistent, reliable, immutable promise I offer. She's gamed the system by figuring out a way to manipulate authenticity.

These fools out here aren't blameless, though. It's been said that I can be stark, plain, and brutal when necessary, but it's how I'm made, and maybe that's too inflexible for people today. Maybe that's why people turn their backs on what's real and go find someone who'll say and do whatever it is they feel makes them matter in the moment. If you're not in a relationship with someone who's real, why should you need to be your true self?

I remember when the words *to thine own self be true* warned that we should act and think with our virtue in mind. Now, I think, the phrase, like a meditation, has become a mantra people play on repeat until they walk away newly enlightened, acting and thinking in their own best interests above all else. That's more of her work right there. I guarantee it.

I learned this the hard way when I dated a guy whom I thought to be honorable. Turns out Honor was just one of the many masks he wore to present his tailor-made self to me. I don't know about the women who came before, but I have a low tolerance for deception, which he soon found out, but I digress. Masks have never been my thing after all because I *am* Truth. I cannot tell a lie. Literally. I can't even fudge when it comes to what's right, so it amazes me as I watch people pick up and cast away personas and behaviors with precision, cloaking their bare essence with actions, peccadillos, and habits that they've deliberately distilled from some YouTube video or TV show until they learn to affect an aura or attitude that they like better. Think VSCO girls. When you need a brand and don't like your own, copy something proven to go viral. Like smallpox. I feel like I'm surrounded by aliens and changelings who've shifted what it means to step out of character now that you literally can do this at will. More than that, and in a fundamental way, I wonder if all of this means that Deceit is the new normal. But let's leave that for another day.

I think the thing that gets me the most is that I'm having this internal discussion in the first place. Some things don't change; saying that they have doesn't make it so. I can't help but wonder if somewhere behind the scenes a seismic shift left her in charge. Maybe Influence turned everything on its ear just enough that we awoke the next morning questioning everything we thought to be true a mere eight hours earlier.

Who am I kidding?! That would require planning and strategy, and for that, I can't bring myself to give her any credit whatsoever. I mean, look at her! And then look at me. I'm not one to brag, but a poet I once knew paid me the highest compliment. Though I admit I'm not all that hard on the eyes, the dear young man, who was quite the romantic, caused a bit of a stir when he declared that I *am* beauty, that we're one and the same, pure, and constant, never ceasing. It wasn't a pick-up line, but from what I could tell, young John was emotionally intense and felt everything quite deeply – in the moment. He also was obsessed with death, so I always resisted any deep connection with that one. Now, I do hope you'll pardon my tangent, but it goes quite well to my point: Where's the literary masterpiece she inspired? Where is the good in what she represents? Who's relying on her to bring consistency?

More likely, then, I wonder if there might have been a catastrophic mutation in relationship DNA, leaving its foundation on a precarious single-helix structure, wobbly, inconstant, and unable to thrive. Lacking the common ground required to prop up the tenuous passion, it dies out, I guess. Could that be why Unpredictability and Inconsistency are a lot easier to find than Constancy and Loyalty? Or are some people simply made not to care? No matter how many times you show them your heart, they can't see past their own whims and desires. It doesn't seem that hard to do what you say you'll do, to mean what you say, or to say what you feel. But maybe some people just aren't born to see anything beyond what the mirror reflects even when I'm standing right there alongside.

So, for now, as these uncertainties loom and spell doom for my interactions, I've decided to take a break from relationships, at least until I find someone who can see beyond his own hype and be real with me.

I know that I can be demanding. I know it's tough to face the very things that make us loathe to see ourselves clearly. But I assure you I am more than worth any pain or discomfort you might feel on the way to enlightenment. Because I can show you better than I can tell you, I'd like to share a story of what happens when two people find each other and inner peace as they embrace truth. Masks must be shed, and paths must be discovered before they can find their way forward. And though they will find their way, rest assured, it's not quite that neat and clean, it being the course of true love and all. When relics from our past resurface, we must find a way to reconcile their records and any hurts they leave behind before returning them to their proper place in our memories. After that, of course, lessons get learned, and lives can be lived happily ever after. The thing about happily ever after? You're bound to pick up a battle scar or ten on the way to bliss. So, sit back, take heed, and take note. The story that I'm about to unfold is near to my heart, so there are bound to be a few lessons baked in here.

Act One: The Well-Intentioned White Lie

Chapter 1

Saturday, August 17
Mateo

THE SUN PEEKS TIMIDLY from behind one of the many fluffy pinkish-white masses floating lazily across the early morning sky. It's Saturday, just past 7 a.m., and I'm having second thoughts about what, until now, had seemed like an ingenious idea. As I slow my Ducati, my mind skims through the possible scenarios that could unfold over the next minutes. I pull into one of the many parking spaces that skirt the entrance to the Loudoun County, Virginia, park where I'll be spending the next two hours training with the Renegade Running Club. I kill the throaty motor, peel off my helmet, and comb through my hair and my resolve one final time.

I've never been one to indulge in self-doubt or self-recrimination. I know what I want, and I'm used to pursuing whatever that is unapologetically. *So why the hell does it feel like I'm about to jump a cliff?*

In two words: Alexa Winston.

I can't shake the heavy deliberation that weighs me down as I grab the duffle bag stored in the space beneath my seat and walk across the lot to the recreation center. A gentle breeze shoots a welcome rush of air through my helmet-crushed hair, and I run my hand through the mess once more to try to bring some order to what the wind has destroyed before I enter the building. Taking a deep breath and gathering my resolve, I scout for a restroom where I can trade my jeans, boots, and leather jacket for the running gear I picked up last night.

There's great irony in this when you consider that running interests me about as much as owning a Chia pet. Sure, I stay in shape, so it's not the running that has me on edge. But this is *her* passion, so I need to make it appear to be mine as well if I want her to take this little shenanigan seriously, if I want her to stop deflecting and take me seriously. Not so long ago, the notion that I would ever consider something resembling a relationship was laughable. Even sillier

INTERMEZZO: THE INTERLUDES

now is the fact that I have only myself to blame for my current relationship status with this enigmatic, golden-eyed beauty.

From our first meeting nearly a year ago, I'd been drawn to her – and not just in the way I regard most women these days. The attraction between us was instant, but it was more than just that. Our conversation came easy. The connection was clear and though it was intimidating, it didn't stop me from pursuing her. At first, she deflected my advances. That made her a challenge to me, but challenge quickly transformed into fascination. We struck up a friendship, a brand-new experience for me because I don't do well with women friends. They typically end up wanting more than I'm willing to give, but that wouldn't be the case with Alexa. I've spent the past many months learning this woman, courting her, really, though I don't like to think of it in such romantic, outdated terms. A fellow relationship refugee, Alexa fears our growing intimacy, which keeps us stuck in an interesting no-fly zone in our relationship. Our friendship is tight, true, and undeniable. The bond we've built is thick and apparently evident when we're together. Yet, we've found ourselves stranded at an interesting outpost and can't seem to move ahead on our journey.

Like I said, though, much of this is on me. For the past ten years, my heart has had no use for the fairer sex, well, not beyond sex anyway. When you're out here like that, it doesn't go unnoticed. But I never gave a shit. Not until I met her. Something about Alexa is different, true. She's goodness and light. Trouble is, she views me through a single lens – because that's the only way I'd wanted her to see me at first. I flirted, teased, and laced much of my early interactions with her with innuendo. It was easier that way. I knew she wouldn't call my bluff, and it gave me time to understand better what I was feeling for her and why it was so different. For a short while, that had been fine with me ... until it wasn't. Until I could no longer deny that friendship was only part of what I wanted with her.

So, I went and did the unthinkable. Having slept with more women than I can ever account for, it was no great sacrifice to abstain for a while. It hadn't been a conscious decision really, but I haven't had a woman in my bed since shortly after meeting Alexa, so do the math. I knew my heart had overtaken my head the first time I deflected an offer for hot, sweaty, no-strings-attached sex from a cute undergraduate in one of the psychology classes I teach at American University. Then, with the next offer I'd declined one night while out trolling with friends, I realized shit had gotten serious. The university has long been one of my most lucrative playgrounds for hooking up, but I've had enough of the empty, hollow feeling that visits me and hangs around after a mindless romp in the sack. And though something more means something quite scary, the idea of a future with Alexa gives me a hope I haven't felt in a long time.

So, slowly, and with focused deliberation, I've become a man with a plan. After some successful Facebook and Instagram stalking, I learned that Alexa is an avid runner. In measured steps over the last few months, I've chatted her up about the hobby, all but convincing her that this is yet another common thread to bind the friendship we share.

Even though I've sown some fertile seeds with Alexa, I've sensed her tensing and retreating as our attraction has begun showing signs of an intimacy and attachment that hasn't previously been there. I still need to find my way in, which is what brings me here to begin training for the Prospect Park Classic Distance Duathlon – a 10-mile bike ride through the storied Brooklyn park sandwiched between two 5K runs. This will be my lever. And so, I'll train with her (coincidentally, of course), forcing us to spend time together outside of our professional personas so we won't be able to deny the pull between us anymore.

I find a strange sense of comfort in these thoughts as I exit the bathroom and head toward the center of the lobby where the group has begun assembling. No way could she freak out when she sees me, right? But I won't have a chance to debate with myself over this. Before either of us can avoid it, Alexa, who's just finished tying her running shoes, bounds up without looking, sending her careening into my chest. I grab her shoulders to halt her momentum.

"Hey, hang on there, freight train! What's your rush?"

Chapter 2

Alexa

FREIGHT TRAIN, INDEED. Only I feel like I've been hit by one when my mind deciphers who and what I've just collided into.

Oh. The Hell. No.

In what seems like slo-mo replay, my eyes travel up the well-muscled chest that blocks my path until they meet his gorgeous face. In truth, I didn't need to see the face to know the identity of the solid object in my path. The smell, the voice. The dreamy gray-green eyes that make me think of the Caribbean and see straight through to my soul. It was Mateo Da Rocha in glorious 4k right in front of my face. Quite literally.

I draw in a quick, shallow breath, planting my hands on his forearms while trying to find my voice. "Mateo? What are you doing here?"

Still holding on to my shoulders, he gives a slight squeeze before bending down to kiss my cheeks European style. "I could ask you the same," he teases, deliberately bypassing my question. That doesn't go unnoticed.

"A duathlon seems a bit too badass for you, Lexi," he smiles, which for some reason makes me blush and knocks me off-center. He's not exactly wrong in his assessment because this will be the longest, most intense race I've entered to date. But he doesn't need to know this, so I throw my shoulders back and strut my moxie.

"Then it looks like you don't know what I'm capable of, Da Rocha." I'm still struggling for my composure, cursing myself as I try to put away the assortment of way-too-awkward feelings that completely arrests my body and my brain. Hastily, I find my smile, put a mask back in place, and try not to consider the possibility that steam might be pouring from my ears if my rushing heartbeat is any indicator of such things.

"Seriously, what in the world brings you all the way out here? Aren't you operating a little outside of your area code?"

He laughs, and I'm grateful for the unintended ice breaker I'd thrown out there.

"You really need to lose the idea that my address somehow limits where I can go and what I should do, Alexa. But now let me ask *you* a question. Why do you assume I don't have ties around here?"

"A fair question. I didn't consider that. My bad," I answer with as much indifference as I can muster. Something about him, about our interactions, has been shifting over the past weeks. I can't put my finger on exactly what it is. No, that's a lie. The connection between us has been strong since we met. But I'm too afraid to go there with him and ruin our friendship and maybe risk my heart again. I take a small step back, just enough to pull away from Mateo's lingering grasp on my shoulders. But the space between us remains saturated with our shared tension.

"So, seriously, what brings you out to God's country? No running clubs in DC?" I need to do something to break the bonds of this intensity between us.

He folds his arms across his chest and smiles. "I have some connections nearby."

"Oh, hey, I had no idea," I say. "So, I guess you get out here a fair bit then."

I've noticed that most of the time, when asked, Mateo prefers to be vague about the details of his life. I've wondered what secrets he may be hiding but chalked it up more to caution than anything else. We aren't too different when it comes to our willingness or not to trust the opposite sex.

"Often enough."

"What's that mean? Care to 'splain?"

"No, love. No, I don't. At least not today," he says with a wink. "What do you say we get settled in here and figure out just what we've gotten ourselves into," he deflects as he nods to the registration desk to his left. "I haven't checked in yet—"

"Mateo, you ass, you can't do that!" I chide him playfully. "You can't just leave me hanging."

"Sure, I can. I just did," he says with that panty-dropping smile. "Now come on. Let's go do this thing."

My jaw drops as Mateo turns away from me and heads over for his registration papers. As he takes his place in line, I catch up to him and tug his forearm.

"You're seriously not going to tell me?"

"Of course, I will. Just not now," he teases. "In fact, it'll be my leverage."

"Leverage?" I ask.

"Uh huh. My way of ensuring you'll agree to train with me. Share in this insane experience with me, and I'll tell you...soon." His smile grows as he reads the obvious confusion on my face. In answer, he points to a sign on the table: Designate your intended training partner at time of sign up.

My face drops as I process what this would mean. Running is my sanctuary, a sacred place where my thoughts and I can be alone and in step, whether at peace or in discord. I don't share that with anyone. *But how can I say no to him? How can I deny that this makes my heart beat faster than any foot race?* I swallow to relieve the dryness in my throat as I slowly, reluctantly but with moth-to-a-flame resignation realize this truth. I *can't* say no to him. Not that he's ever asked anything of me. Not really. But now ...?

"Well," I begin carefully, speaking more to myself than to him, "I guess there's a first time for everything." I wait a beat while he considers my words. This was a compromise, a convenient compromise. It was *not* about the fact that I can't tell him no or that I'm scared for us be alone like that. "So sure, let's partner up. Though full disclosure: I have no idea what that means. Trying to train with someone, I mean."

"Well, then, I guess we're perfectly matched because I don't have a clue either. No expectations. No pressure, right?" Mateo raises his eyebrows expectantly. I can tell that he can tell that I'm not wholly comfortable with his proposal, and if I'm not mistaken, this seems to please him. Ignoring his satisfaction and resisting the mounting urge to cut and run, I simply nod, square my shoulders, and feign my resolve.

"So, it's settled. *Now* what?"

"No clue," he says, "but we should probably figure it out fast. We're next up." And with that, he eases me around in front of him, slips his right palm into the small of my back, and guides me up to the desk to sign on for twelve weeks of Lord only knows what.

Some 20 minutes later, Mateo and I have joined 16 of our new closest friends as we warm up and listen to our instructor run down the highlights and goals of the training program. Our coach, Linzi, gives off a pixie-like energy and is *way* too perky for my liking. Though she's attractive enough, she's going to be nothing but annoying as hell, all five-feet-two inches of her. Her blonde bob cut, straight, white teeth thanks to thousands of dollars in orthodontia, and cheerleader-like demeanor can't make up for the fact that, for me, she's already an irritant. I work like it's my job to contain the urge to get the hell out of there as pixie-faced Linzi drones on and on about the ultimate challenge that our bodies would be facing.

"I promise you," she begins her wrap-up pep talk, "that if you all push yourselves to the limit and follow this program like your lives depend on it, you will have experienced nothing, and I mean nothing, any more exhilarating than the feeling you get when you finish your first duo."

If her trite take on life's best moments is any indication, Little Miss Linzi is not only shy of a brain cell or two but clearly hasn't experienced enough life to make such a call. So, by the time she finally directs the training pairs to run our first 5K, at least five minutes later, aiming for a slow, steady pace, I'm more than ready to beat feet, get out on the road, and pound out a few good miles.

And that's exactly what I do.

Chapter 3

Alexa

I MET MATEO NEARLY a year ago when my dear friend, Sage Vanucci, asked me to be a guest panelist at an annual symposium of working journalists, professors, and affiliated professionals from the advertising and communications communities. Sage is managing editor at the *Washington Post* and founder of "The Death of Journalism and the Rise of Information Domination," a three-day conference which has become the place to be each spring when purveyors of knowledge and curators of content gather to speak their truths, whether or not they're actually knowledgeable or simply exploiting their popularity as influencers within the digital wasteland that is social media. The whole thing was more about the quotes and quips that get shuttled around through Tweets and shares, cool Insta photos, and TikTok videos. Still, it was one of the few conference destinations remaining where the buzz that charged the room surpassed any buildup orchestrated within the cybersphere, which was precisely what Sage envisioned when he conceived the event.

Sage basically pestered his panels into place, calling on friends new and old as well as personalities he'd yet to charm with his wit and charisma. As his long-time friend and confidante, no hadn't been an option for me. Sage and Mateo, however, share more of a passing acquaintance and keep each other at arm's length. At best, they nurture a love-hate relationship and tend to circle each other like vultures vying for a fresh kill.

From the start, Mateo and I shared a palpable attraction and a mutual curiosity about each other that felt as vital as air. But never one to believe in insta-love, soul-deep connections, or any of the ethereal notions associated with matters of the heart, I've made it my business to shut Mateo down. It's not that I'm not interested. I've had more than my fair share of colorful fantasies about the man. And that's why I insist on keeping a bright line between us; he defies logic – and threatens my thread-bare defenses against him – in every way.

Just shy of twenty-five minutes later, I finish my first shared run. It didn't suck.

Mateo and I had wordlessly kept the same cadence for much of our time out on the trail. Except for the occasional "heads up" and brief "on your right," we hadn't spoken since we took off along one of the many scenic asphalt trails that spirals throughout and around the picturesque facility. I'd been certain that this desecration of my solitude was of the devil. Then, I got over myself and considered the facts. The training group required that you train in pairs. Had I not paired with Mateo, I'd have been stuck with some uber competitive female I probably couldn't have stood to be around, or worse, a weekend warrior-type with self-worth issues and/or sociopathic tendencies. Or maybe both knowing my luck.

No, the experience was not at all what I'd expected. Not only had I found a surprising peace and satisfaction in our shared silence, but after a little more than three miles together in each other's space, I also somehow feel closer to this man who does strange things to my stomach just by being around. He is six-feet-three inches of beautifully sculpted, solid, gorgeous, ripped, lean muscle. The way he moves and his long, self-assured, sensual strides command respect, attention, and admiration. He'd contained his silky black hair, which falls to his shoulders, in a ponytail that was wet at the tips from exertion, and based on his half-erect stance and still-rolling sweat, I realize with satisfaction that I've outrun him.

He gropes at the hem of his shorts as I walk toward the imposing willow oak tree that sheltered our essentials while we ran. When I reach the pink canvas duffle bag that my oldest son, Tristan, gave me for my last birthday, I root around for water and a fresh shirt. At first, I hadn't been keen on walking around carrying a bag emblazoned with the words "queen energy" in bright blue letters. It was almost impossible to deny Tristan, though. My oh-so-disaffected teen had been so proud to bless me with cool merch (his words), and I hadn't wanted to hurt the boy's feelings. After finding the courage to carry the thing in public over the last weeks, I've actually grown fond of the silly thing and the conversation it inspired. I smile at the thought as I take another long swallow of water.

By now, Mateo is on his way over, sufficiently recovered, it seems, from a few moments ago. I hold out my water bottle as he ducks under a low-hanging branch to join me at the base of the tree. He nods and huffs out a breathy, "thanks," accepting the bottle graciously and chugging the remaining half of its contents. I giggle as I watch him slake what must have been the thirst of a lifetime. Then, I slip around to the other side of the massive, old tree for a bit of cover while I trade my soaked gray racerback for a fitted camouflage printed tee.

"So, tell me, Mateo, you seemed a little off your pace today. No?"

"No, not at all, Lex." *Fucking liar. This chick damn near killed you!* "But I'm afraid I am quite distracted today."

I reappear from my makeshift dressing room, a frown of confusion across my brow. "Why distracted? What's up?" I ball up the sweaty shirt to dab my misty brow as I walk over to rejoin him.

Mateo

What I'm about to tell her probably won't help in my crusade to get this girl to take me seriously. But I can't help myself. Truth is truth. Besides I find it curiously satisfying that I can rattle her. It's like she inspires the 13-year-old boy in me to show his awkward face around the equally awkward, unbearably, intimidatingly cute girl he wants to ask out.

"Your legs."

She stares at me as she processes what I've said. After a few moments, she narrows her eyes and tilts her head slowly to the left in question just as I wave her off and flash a quick wink along with the smile that I know fries women's brains. I'm not necessarily trying to flirt my way into her heart, and this tack isn't going to be productive in my crusade to change the course of our relationship. It's my natural default. And because I've let the genie out, I might as well see if charm can at least unlock the vault that guards her defenses.

"You heard me, girl," I drawl, stalking over to close the remaining space between us. "I said it's your legs. They're what's distracting me." I tilt my head to mirror hers and point casually towards the source of my lost focus.

Alexa squares her shoulders, standing just a bit taller as she peers up at me through bewildered eyes. I can't tell what she's thinking, but her breathing seems to pick up pace, and her eyes scan mine, searching for the truth. After far too long, she opens her mouth to reply, and I place a finger across her lips.

"Hey, I know that was from left field," I offer, lifting the finger from her lips to brush her cheek with a whisper-soft touch that creates gooseflesh along her arms. *Noted.* "But the way you move when you run, it's amazing." My eyes hold hers captive as we stand but a hair's breadth apart. "You're strong. You're clever. And you're sexy as all hell, Lexi." *Ok, lunatic. So much for taking it slow.*

My words seem to anchor her in place, and I know she must feel the irresistible force drawing us dangerously closer both physically and emotionally. She finally breaks my gaze after a few precious moments, clears her throat, and sadly takes a couple of steps away, leaving me feeling strangely wanting and needful.

"Da Rocha," she says, a slight plea in her voice, "you must be delirious. I don't know what you think you just saw—"

"What I saw is your grace and strength on full display," I pause, crossing my arms across my chest and letting my eyes wander to her lean, well-muscled thighs. "The way you move in those tall heels you're always wearing doesn't even begin to do you justice. The whole time we were out there, you and those gorgeous legs kept me off my pace, off my game, nearly drove me out of my mind with distraction."

She clears her throat once more and dips her head to hide her blush. "Then you need your eyes checked, Da Rocha. And maybe you need a different training partner if you're so easily, um, *distracted.*"

Again, I close the distance between us and reach for her strong, toned shoulders, giving them a quick, playful squeeze. "No, I think I'm right where I want to be, thank you. I'll make do somehow." I walk past her to the base of the tree, bend down to snatch up my duffle, then return to fill up her personal space once again. "And my eyes are just fine, Alexa." I give her a small smile and let her consider my words.

She's confounded and intrigued and probably doesn't know what to make of the past few moments. But, because I'm coming to know this intoxicating creature quite well, I'll predict her next move: deflection.

"Glad to hear it," she says, returning my smile. "But maybe we should have your head examined just to be sure." She punches me playfully in the arm, hoping to have dismissed the emotional insanity that my flirtation aroused. It may seem counterintuitive, but this brings me considerable satisfaction in my ability to read her thoughts and instincts. "In the meantime," she says, turning to walk away, "we should go back and check in with the pixie stick."

"Pixie stick?"

"Yeah. Linzi."

I laugh heartily at Alexa's nickname for the young girl. "Why, Lex? Why pixie stick?"

"Isn't it obvious?" She asks, a mischievous glint in her eyes as we continue walking back to the rec center. "First off, runner or not, no one's that bubbly at 7 o'clock in the morning. And truth be told, I've never been fond of the perky, blonde cheerleader type."

I nod and shrug my response. "So, it's woman shit, then."

She shakes her head, a little miffed at my dismissal. "No, I think it's human nature. Think about it." She angles herself to look at me as we near our destination. "Two men size each other up. There's something between you that puts one or the other off. You immediately decide you don't like the other guy. It's just a vibe. But it happens all the time. So much more so for women."

"You may be right, Lex," I say, angling in as she had moments before and bending towards her left ear. "But that vibe doesn't set most men on a course for revenge."

"Who said anything about revenge?" she retorts with a shrug. "That would take too much time and interest. I just don't like her. She makes my ass itch."

I laugh again. "And ass itching is a bad thing I take it?"

"The worst," she says, giggling, reaching over to tug on my right arm until my ear is inches from her mouth. "Like a plague attacking from the inside out."

"And God forbid such a plague be allowed to run amok in one's ass," I reply, turning as I speak, my face mere inches from hers.

It's Alexa's turn to erupt in laughter, but before she gets the chance to reply, Linzi squeals in delight, "Well, now, aren't you two just the coziest critters on Earth!" Her annoying voice rings out and seems to reverberate, turning previously disinterested heads towards us as we reunite with the group. "Now, really, am I going to have to separate you two? Did you get in your run at all? You both look much too beautiful."

I take a step forward as if to shield Alexa from Linzi. "I assure you we ran. It wasn't at the slow pace you suggested." I look at Alexa briefly before continuing. "So, we had a little more cool-down time perhaps. Hope that's no issue for you?" I pose my question to the group and find nothing short of keen disinterest.

"None at all," she quickly replies, showing off as many of her 32 teeth as she can squeeze into her shit-eating grin. "I encourage each of you to make your training sessions your own! Now, here's your homework for next week. Every good duathlete needs to challenge their speed threshold to build endurance and, well, to just make the run plain ol' fun."

Alexa and I share a telepathy of sorts, and as she glances at me with obvious disdain for our trainer, I sense with pure clarity what she's feeling for this woman but keep my face unreadable, save the brief wink that most would have missed. We're distracted from our telepathic tête-à-tête when Linzi turns towards a petite young woman who's struggling to hide her own disdain, boredom, or maybe both.

"You just hold on there for a few more moments now, sugarplum," Linzi says, brightening her smile even more as she reaches out to playfully slap at the air between her and the young woman. "I'll have you on your way to that latte you must have skipped this beautiful mornin'."

A few pairs of previously disinterested eyebrows raise among the group members at the small rebuke.

"So, as I was saying, you and your partner need to get together this week and plan your tempo runs. Be thoughtful about this before you do it so you can challenge yourselves, and I'll see all you early birdies back here next Saturday." She waves both of her hands at the group as she backs away and eventually turns her back in dismissal.

In rapid response, the group disperses with the speed and urgency of animals seeking higher ground in the wake of the next Great Flood. I nudge Alexa and nod my head in the direction of the parking lot. "I've got an idea. Come." I fall into pace just slightly behind her, gently guiding her steps with my right hand, which is comfortably wedged into that space just above her nicely rounded ass. It's a soft, subtle pressure that seems to shift her senses into hyper drive, which is exactly why I do it. Every muscle in her body seems to strain towards my touch, and though I see her turn slightly to look at me in question, I keep my gaze trained straight ahead. Just as she's about to fidget around and away from my touch, I move my hand to her left arm and tug her to a stop.

"Are you in a hurry?"

A question forms on her brow as she slowly shakes her head no.

"Good. Then have breakfast with me." I see the question in her eyes deepen followed by something that looks a lot like fear. In the time we've been hanging out, having a meal together isn't all that unusual, though it's typically been at least loosely related to our work. Meeting for coffee to make a pros and cons list when she got her job at the PR firm. Inviting her to guest lecture my classes followed by drinks. The calls and texts. Each interaction feels a bit more intimate than the last, intensifying the pull between us, which is fine by me. But her natural inclination is to run from that and from me, and this needs to change. I put these thoughts aside for now and rush to close the deal because I see the rebuff forming on her tongue. "I don't bite. *Not too hard anyway.* But you should know that by now, Lex."

I can see that my grand un-plan to blur the lines of our relationship is falling the hell to pieces before it even gets going, and I have only myself to blame. I've never really given her more than a glimpse of myself. She has no idea who I am in sum. I remain cloaked, for the most part, operating in panty-drop mode, my smile inviting, albeit rakish, but sincere to the common observer (which Alexa is not). Tempting yet full of warning. So, I can't and shouldn't have expected a reaction other than the one in front of me. I surprise myself with my response to that notion. The instinct to mask my own insecurities and hurts lives deep inside each cell, etched both genetically and behaviorally on my soul. I table these thoughts as I pull at her elbow slightly, giving it a nearly imperceptible squeeze. "Hey, it's just breakfast. Completely safe." I step away a little, holding up both of my hands as a sign of peace. "The best breakfast you've ever had. Hands down."

She smiles, but uncharacteristically, I can't tell what's on her mind because she's expertly masked herself, which pisses me off – royally.

"Sounds good. Sign me up."

Though I'm still feeling the sting of her having shut off her emotions, I return her smile as she turns away and calls over her shoulder as casually as possible, faux smile locked in place, "I'll just get my truck. Lead the way."

Alexa

"...the best breakfast you've ever had. Hands down."

I'd searched my brain for a polite rejection but could find none. Instead, it was painfully clear that my faculties no longer had jurisdiction here because I was completely focused on what my heart and body obviously want. *I wonder what it would feel like with your hands down my...*

Certain that my dirty thoughts would grow little feet and dash over into his brain, I'd turned as swiftly as I could to hide my face and head towards my SUV. About 20 minutes later, we arrive at our destination, but I am no less shaky than I'd been when I agreed to go with him. Aptly named, The Breakfast Nook is tucked well out of sight, solidly off a well-traveled thoroughfare that bisects Middleburg, Virginia. The quaint hamlet oozes the image that Loudoun County craves and trades on. A bedroom community nestled in the ultra 'burbs, quite well west of Washington, DC, the median income is more than twice that of most other places in the nation. Its resources are abundant, and the communities are precisely engineered, offering all the components required to meet and exceed the ideal of the American Dream.

Mateo slices his motorcycle into one of the shoebox-sized spaces without effort. I, on the other hand, seem to have forgotten how to park as I watch him tear off his helmet, shake out his hair, and dismount the mammoth bike. It really isn't fair that I have so much trouble resisting my connection to him. *We are just friends, and this is just breakfast. We are just friends, and this is just breakfast.* I chant silently to myself as I train my focus on the optics and away from the man. It's a stupid meal, for heaven's sake, I remind myself as I maneuver my midnight blue BMW X5 through a ridiculously tight lane that opens (but just slightly) to a sad little parking lot with crackled asphalt backing the restaurant. But that's just it. It really isn't just breakfast. This is a tipping point, following months of interest, curiosity, and fascination, which for me has become a primal desire that I can't indulge. At least, I won't let myself indulge it. My marriage taught me all about the vulnerable underbelly of a relationship. How small wounds left to fester and ooze undetected can eat away at your vital parts until you no longer recognize what's left or what you've become. My divorce brought comfort and restored my life. I know this. And yet, I find myself falling deeper into Mateo. Wanting more than I know how to handle. I swear as my resolve to resist him melts away with whatever is left of the concentration that I seem to need to ease my truck between these too-tight lines. Looks like whoever owns this lot has a passion for compact cars only.

I look up from this parking fuckery to see Mateo standing to the side observing my vehicular struggle with poorly masked glee. Yet, I can swear I see arousal radiating from him in pulsing waves, washing over me and frying my brain. Stopping my heart. He crosses his arms against his broad chest and trains his eyes on mine. He knows he's rattling me and seems rather pleased with himself. But I can't care about that just now. I watch as his amusement shifts back to desire, which makes my cheeks grow hot. Damn him!

After what seems like much too long, I shut off the engine and reach over to grab my purse from the passenger seat. I ease open the door and squeeze through the narrow passage. As I make my way to him, I'm again undeniably captivated by his presence. To say he's handsome is wholly inadequate. Smoky green-gray eyes, a striking complement to his olive/tan, sun-kissed skin, remind me of jade and feature flecks of amber and sunshine, rendering them focused, penetrating, and hypnotic. But he isn't just unbelievably attractive. He's charismatic. He towers over most people in every way ... and not just because of his height. It's hard to ignore his presence and power, which not only seem to draw people near, but also aid him in reading and deciphering their motivations. I should know because the man breaks me down with just a sideways glance. I'll never admit it, but I suspect I don't have to.

Yes, Dr. Mateo Da Rocha, Psy. D., is a delicious, lust-filled fantasy. This friendship I thought we could have is real and rich. But it's become so much more than that as he continues burrowing his way into my life and heart. I shake myself back to reality as I mentally pour cold water onto this treacherous mix of arousal and panic vying for my full attention.

Mateo

Over the next hour and a half, we enjoy our breakfast as I pry my way into this beauty's life. Alexa is light, goodness, and all kinds of sexy. I swear her eyes flash at me with what only can be a described as a promissory note for lose-your-heart sex. And I'm sure she doesn't even know it. Looking into her golden-brown-and-amber eyes is like staring into the sun longer than you should. You know how you see those floaty circles of light afterwards? Just like that, it blinds me when I look at her, and that scares the crap out of me. For real. It's like a flame that promises to scald me to the core, but I can't resist getting closer to it. I need to feel this heat. Once I thought that I could fuck her out of my system, but I can't go there. A random, mindless encounter could never scratch this itch. Instead, I've been breaking her down slowly, gently, bringing her around to realize this until she's forced to submit to the connection we share. My sudden interest in running is probably my best opportunity to bring her around to my way of thinking, so it's time to make a strategic move.

"So," I begin once our table is cleared of dishes and we sit sipping cups of the best coffee in the charted universe, "how should we tackle our training?"

She purses her lips but doesn't respond immediately. I know her well enough at this point that I can almost see her brain at work, but on what, I can't say. Not saying I'm a mind reader. But I assess people with near precision whether they want me to or not. Getting at Alexa has always been a much tougher hack.

"Are you sure you want to do this, Da Rocha?"

"Of course. Why wouldn't I?"

"I don't know. You didn't exactly seem to be at home on the trails," she says. It's more a challenge than a statement, but I'm not taking that bait. When I don't respond, she lets some of her frustration show. "Look, stop shitting me. This is the only training club you could find?"

There are lots of ways to play this. Did I figure she'd figure me out? Of course. Did I think she'd call me on it immediately? Hell no. She's not pissed, but I'll need to be careful. A little white lie never hurt anyone. There was no bad intent or malice behind my ruse. I could come clean on that, and I probably should. But I also think I need a way to turn this to my advantage. While I figure out what that is, I'll buy myself some time.

"The only one? No, of course not. But it's the one with the best view."

"See, that right there," she says, pointing a well-manicured finger my way, "you want me to believe—"

"I want you to believe in what you feel."

This sums up our dilemma in simplest terms. I may flirt with her on purpose, but I do it for a few reasons. I can admit that I enjoy how she reacts when I do, but more important, it keeps her focused on what's between us, the proverbial elephant in the room that she keeps trying to ignore. She's been fighting herself to find her reasons to say no because she won't, can't, doesn't want to trust in what we could be. I don't know which. I don't even know if that's the only reason for her resistance. I just need to remove all the whys from her mind and replace them with why not.

"Let's say hypothetically that I arranged our chance meeting hoping to give us more time together. Your life demands order, so what better way to find more time with you than to schedule it in with something you'd planned on doing since you won't give us a chance to explore what this is." I laugh, and it's appropriately naked and self-deprecating. Somehow, though, I feel lighter having rid my brain of the words. "I can think of a lot worse things I could do, so that wouldn't really be considered shitting you, now would it?"

She gives me a smile that makes my knees unsteady while she considers me much like a teacher does a clever, mischievous student. "Well, it doesn't make you a lying liar that lies. But you obviously have an angle."

This might be the time to fold. How I show this hand matters, though. I may use fun and flirty as my default setting, but she needs to understand that I'm serious – about her, about us, about learning more about what us means even if I can't quite be sure I know that myself just yet. "I need to peel back the rest of your layers, Lexi. But I'm willing to earn the right to what I want."

She studies me with interest and a little apprehension, too. "And that is?"

I shake my head, amused but a bit frustrated as she holds my feet to this fire. "You know what I want, love. You want it, too, because if you didn't, you'd shut me down completely. But you don't. So, the question is why you keep resisting. That's one of the things I want to know." I stand from my bench across from her and motion for her to move over so I can slide in beside her. I lean forward to close the space between us even more and reach for her hand, stroking her fingers absently. "But there are other things, too. So, for the next few weeks, we'll play a game. Let's call it The Reason Why Not."

"What's with you and games?" She laughs but it's a fair question. It may even be one of the reasons she prefers to believe I'm not all that serious about getting her to change her mind considering that I've hit her with a couple of these made-up gems of mine over the months.

"They're fun and non-threatening," I answer her finally. "But that's not the question you need to be asking."

She groans and gives me a reluctant smile. "I'll probably regret this, but what should I be asking?"

"You need to know how the game will work, love. So here it is: We'll play for a few weeks. At the beginning of each week, as we set our training goals for the race, of course, we set a goal to help fill in one huge blank about each other. When we share what we learned at the end of the week, that moves us one step closer to an actual date. Four weeks. Four new reasons to tell me yes."

"You're a smug, SOB, Da Rocha. Even if it's yes," she sighs, "the answer still has to be no." She smiles and relaxes but just slightly, thinking she's won.

"Think so?" I counter, all in for the challenge because I'm more certain than ever that what she's feeling is something very different from what she wants me to believe.

"I've told you this." There's something sad and conflicted in her eyes, which is a new feature to this on-repeat conversation. I nod as I try to decide if I like this look on her.

"You have. Still not listening, though." And now seems like a good time to close this out before she finds her way out. "We usually hang out some each week anyway, so it won't be like adding something completely new to the schedule. We'll just have a bit more ground to cover when we're together. We'll work out the rest as the weeks go on. Sound like a plan?"

"No," she answers quickly with a panicked laugh, "I haven't agreed to play your game, Da Rocha."

"But you won't say no."

"Mateo," she searches my eyes, her own pleading and desperate, "I'll never deny that there's an ease between us, and it's unlike anything I've ever experienced. I'm drawn to you, sure, and that's all good, but I don't know if that's enough to sustain a relationship. What's more, it frightens the hell out of me." I silently urge her to continue because so far, I don't see the big issue. This is also the most candid she's been about her feelings. She looks away briefly and closes her eyes like she's steeling herself to say or do something she really doesn't want to. "You could have any woman at all." No sooner do the words rush from her lips that she clamps them shut. She didn't mean to say that last part aloud, but *this*, this simple, vitally important piece of our puzzle, is what has the potential to fuck me up the most unless I can help her navigate past my reputation and begin to see me. The me I want to be with her anyway.

"Apparently not," I counter, "because the one I want can't seem to trust that what I say to her – to *you* – is how I feel. I don't meet women who intrigue me the way that you do. Who are half as beautiful as you. Who are as self-assured and as self-possessed as you. All I'm asking," I grab for her hand and squeeze it because it's time to close this out, "is that you drop your shields and give me the chance to show you that you can trust me and that what we can be together is worth the risk. So, for the next four weeks, no more hiding. No more deflecting."

"Mateo, I don't know if I can—"

"Say yes."

She stares at me for a moment, the fear evident in her golden-brown eyes. Still, somehow, thankfully, she agrees, and after a mini debate over the tab, I settle, and we take off. Let the games begin.

Alexa

I must have lost my whole mind.

I'm having trouble concentrating on my girl's night in as I sit on my patio several hours later sipping what is perhaps my leventieth glass of wine with Belinda Hopkins and Phaedra Sheppard. Belinda, or Lindy, has been my bestie almost since the day we arrived at the University of Virginia, where we shared four years of laughs and tears that lay the foundation for our unyielding friendship. Phaedra and I have a more complex relationship. I often rely on her spectacular event management prowess when I have clients who rely on high-end wining and dining to close deals, make launch announcements, or hold other swanky gatherings because Phae is the queen of making things look and feel big, pretty, and impressive. Outside of work, however, she's more frenemy than friend. While she's brash and bold in her assessment of everything, I tend to look for the common-ground factors, which is why we barely tolerate each other much of the time. But with Lindy as our common bond, we do our best to shield her from our well-reigned contempt for the other. Phae means well, but she also brings fresh interpretation to what it means to damn with faint praise, and it's with that in mind that I arm myself so that I can deal as civilly as I can.

But who am I kidding? Tonight, she could probably insult, curse, and cast elaborate spells on my progeny and me, and I still wouldn't give her the favor of a reply. Since we left breakfast this morning, Mateo has fully occupied the real estate in my mind. He sent his first week's emo challenge, as my brain is calling this insane game, about an hour ago.

Ms. Winston, Tear Down That Wall.
Imagine you've lost the superpower to deflect all week.
You can't mask what you feel.
Only direct, honest reactions can escape once the Amazonium fortress is gone.

Amazonium? The hell? It seems the first round of this imbecilic game will involve three exploration sessions, two impromptu explorations during the week, and one on our scheduled training/hangout day. I'm not sure what to expect but brighten a little to the prospect that he's awaiting my challenge to him.

"Alexa, hello!" Lindy's repeated taps to my forearm eventually bring me back to the present, and I have no idea what I've missed. "What do you think? Do you think you can finally get away for that girl's weekend we've been talking about?"

"Sorry, Lin," I offer with a small shrug. "I zoned out. Got some stuff on my mind. What did I miss?"

"I hope it has something to do with that yummy professor who's trying to nail you," Lindy suggests with a broad smile.

"Yummy professor!? What have I missed?" Phaedra demands.

I wave them both off, not wanting to let either of them inside my head right now. Mateo's whittling away at the last of my defenses. We both know it. Though my self-preservation instincts are screaming at me to cut and run, my heart and body have other ideas.

"It's nothing, Phae."

"It's not nothing, girl, and you know it," Lindy rebukes. "Now come on. Give it up. That man's gotten all in your head and has you up in your feelings when you're supposed to be present and catching up with your girls."

I telegraph my displeasure mostly to Lindy, who knows all too well that I'd rather be beaten than give Phaedra any deeper insights into anything I care about. I sigh and decide to give up a sliver of the truth.

"So, there's this guy, and he's as off-limits for me as he is gorgeous. Today, he showed up at the runner's club I joined, and I agreed to train with him for an upcoming race. I'm having some second thoughts about that and was just working through some things in my head." *Like how the hell I let him talk me into this stupid game with him. But I'll just keep that to myself.*

"Wait, ho, back up," Lindy squeals to me. "He joined your running club? Did you two plan that? Did he just show up?"

"He just showed up," I answer, my voice clipped and strained with the dual frustrations of being forced onto the hot seat and not wanting to offer too much insight when I've yet to make sense of this mishmash of feelings on my own. "But really, don't worry about it. Nothing to see here."

"Sounds like there's a full-length feature film in the making if you're being this cagey about giving up the deets, girl," Phaedra posits. I give her a half smile because we both know she's on to something. We also both know I'll try my best not to cop to it, at least not yet.

"And you did say your Romeo is gorgeous, so what in hell is the problem, Juliet?" Lindy goads. I narrow my eyes at her, my non-verbal promise to kick her ass once we're alone.

"I don't do relationships. You both know this. I may be tempted, but I can't give in. He's not easily put off, though, and it's messing with my head. End of. Now next topic."

Lindy and Phaedra look at each other, their own unspoken conversation blaring their joint disapproval as loudly as a siren. When Lindy looks to me, I shake my head, my warning to her to stop before she crosses a line from which she may not be able to step back. We've known each other too long, been through too much together, for her to goad me into having a conversation I'm not willing or ready to have. Phaedra is guided by a different compass. And when her mouth takes the lead, we usually end up in uncharted waters.

"Alexa, honey," Phaedra begins, her apparent empathy getting my back up, "you can't judge every man you meet by the asswipe that you married. It's not fair to you, and it's definitely not fair to your hottie. There's really only one way to handle this, but you won't know what that is until you do him."

"She's right, you know," Lindy cosigns as she brings her chair closer to mine, her face radiating empathy and compassion. "You're a beautiful, funny, thoughtful woman. It's ok to move on and explore something – some*one* – new. What's the worst that could happen?"

"I get my heart ripped to shreds, that's what!"

"Then this is serious," Phaedra challenges, and I cringe when I spot the gleam in her eyes. "No one said anything about hearts. If you know like I know, you'll let your hormones lead you. Hearts make things messy. So, keep yours out of it, go get with this man and get you some, and everything should be fine."

Here's the thing about advice. It's tough to put stock in it when the offeror carries a dubious worldview – or at least one that you don't or can't subscribe to. Phaedra truly does mean well. She's also in an open marriage and moves through partners like the phases of the moon. As soon as the sex becomes routine, she's off climbing the next guy she fancies. So yeah, she can miss me with her advice.

"Alexa," Lindy interrupts my ruminating, "what are you so afraid of? Dating the man can't hurt you."

My friend knows me so well. I sigh, take a sip of the fruity wine that will linger in the form of a dull headache in the morning, and pour out my fears. Well, some of them at least.

"You know me better than anyone, Lindy. I take lessons from the past seriously. But nothing in my past prepares me for Mateo. The connection is there. The desire is there. Has been since we met. But we're just too different."

"So far, I haven't heard a thing that should hold you back. What am I missing?" Phaedra challenges.

I purse my lips, take yet another sip, and open the floodgate to my true fears. "He's never been married, doesn't have children, and I'm not his usual type, which seems to be a lot younger and less experienced than I am. So, you do the math. We don't add up."

I fear the belly laugh that erupts from Phaedra literally will split her sides, and that puts my shields back up.

"Forget it," I say, returning my glass to the patio table with more force than necessary. I sit back in my chair and close my eyes as I search for the will to keep from throwing them both out so I can go lick my wounded, embarrassed pride.

"Phae, pipe down!" Lindy admonishes, her long box braids whipping around as she shakes her head vigorously at a still-spasming Phaedra. She returns her eyes to me, the understanding there clear and comforting. "You're feeling self-conscious, and you have doubts. I think that's healthy, Alexa. You said he's 36. You're 43. That makes both of you grown-ass, consenting adults. You can't let your fears paralyze you or keep you from being happy. Do you have any reasons to doubt his intentions? I mean, from the little you've shared, it seems that despite your best efforts to shut him down, he's determined to penetrate your sugar walls, babe."

I side-eye my friend before allowing the smirk on my lips to take full bloom. "I hear you, Lin. It's just—" I let my words trail off as I decide whether to take this thought from my head and put it out into the universe. "What I feel for him is so much more than I ever felt for Trent the entire time we were married.

I'm not saying I'm in love with him. But the way Mateo gets me, gets *to* me, the way I understand him, it's like nothing I've ever experienced. I don't know what to do with that. I don't even know if I want to do anything about it."

Phaedra, now recovered from her hysteria, leans forward, and grabs my hands. "Look at me, girl. That's the realest thing I've heard you say so far. And if that's how you feel, who cares how old he is and what his past relationships might have looked like. You won't know what you two might be if you don't take the chance. I don't see what you have to lose."

"Have you both forgotten that I have kids who depend on me as their sole anchor?"

"Yes, you do, and yes, they do. But if you're not happy, then they're not either," Lindy answers, her words stealing the fight clean away from me. "You can tell yourself all day long and twice on Sunday that you're holding back because of your kids, but you won't be doing them any favors in the end. Trust me on this." Though an unplanned pregnancy and a shiftless, deadbeat, eventually drug-addicted baby daddy threatened to derail her Ph.D. studies and her career before it even began, Lindy, with a big assist from yours truly, saw her 17-year-old son, my god son, Luke, through his childhood. He's happy, mature, and well-adjusted, not only because of our love for him, but also because Lindy has always made seeking her happiness a priority, even if it meant getting her feelings hurt or her heart broken. She's modeled what it means to live life on your own terms. And maybe Luke isn't the only one who needs to heed her example.

I eye them both as my mind scrolls through the events of this morning. Hell, if my friends wanted in my business so badly, maybe I should let them dig around so they can help me sort through my confusion.

"Ok, since you two want to play Iyanla Vanzant, then fix my life, heffas. It's not a coincidence that he showed up on the trails this morning."

Phaedra and Lindy look to each other then back to me, their faces prompting me to say more. I sigh and press forward.

"That's just it," I agree. "I know that. And I know what I'd like to think about that. But his say and his do don't always add up for me. We agree more or less that neither of us wants a mindless encounter, yet he's all flirt and little substance most of the time. I don't know him, and that's a problem for me."

"And what does he know about you?" Lindy challenges. "I don't see you exactly putting yourself out there, so have you considered that maybe he feels the same way?"

And that smarted. "I give as good as I get," I bluster with a small shrug.

"So, you'll both remain trapped inside your own twisted, sexually tense version of *Groundhog Day*," Phaedra quips. "You can't find out what you two can be together be if neither of you will take a risk. But today, he took a step to call you both on your bullshit, find out what you do, where you'll be and insert himself into that. It makes me think he's upped the ante. It's your move, precious."

"Maybe," I admit, though I'm still far from being convinced that it's time to go all in.

"Definitely," they say in unison.

"And now that that's settled," Phaedra says, "you need to do the work, Alexa. And in the meantime, let's open another bottle."

About the Author

W ife, mother, daughter, lover of all things literary, Kim Greer has been a storyteller her entire life. From her early days narrating school plays to penning short stories as an angsty pre-teen, Kim's passion for connecting audiences with a good read has bled into all facets of her life. A journalist by training, Kim holds a BA in English Language and Literature from the University of Virginia and an MS in Journalism from Columbia University. She began her communications career as a business reporter for *The Poughkeepsie Journal* and later joined *Crain Communications*, an international publisher of business/trade magazines. In her role with *Crain*, Kim was also a periodic contributor to *Advertising Age*.

After leaving journalism, Kim created and led strategic marketing and communications for several global corporations, helping them to tell their stories and brand their services. In 2008, she launched a boutique marketing consultancy serving clients primarily in the professional services, IT, defense, logistics and aerospace arenas. Concurrently, as an adjunct professor at Georgetown University, she designed and taught PR and communications courses for the school's award-winning graduate program.

Kim lives in northern Virginia with her fabulous husband of nearly three decades, the youngest of their three sons, and Oba, their Rottweiler.

www.ingramcontent.com/pod-product-compliance
Lightning Source LLC
Chambersburg PA
CBHW071321130626
46556CB00004B/1686